FOG MAGIC
Julia L. Sauer

All her life Greta had loved the fog. Her mother said it was unnatural. She herself hated the great gray clouds blowing in from the sea. But somehow a child like Greta was born in every generation of Addingtons, a child who understood the fog. No one knew why—until the day on the old Post Road when the surrey came by with a woman whose plum-colored dress rustled "like a three-master coming up into the wind." The woman was driving toward Blue Cove, and Greta knew that there, where no house had stood for a hundred years, she would find what she was seeking. "Go on," said the woman. "In the second house you'll find Retha Morrill. You two will pull well together."

FOG MAGIC

ACKNOWLEDGMENTS

TO OUR FRIENDS IN LITTLE RIVER

You have made us welcome to the intimate friendliness of your kitchens. As you kneaded your oat bread or as you baited your trawls for the next day's work at sea you have dipped far down into your memories for us and the tales you have told are in themselves like an old road into the past. You have been patient with our endless questions. Always you have made us feel that you knew they sprang from genuine interest rather than curiosity. Some of you have listened to the reading of parts of this story in the lamplit cabin while a silent fog kept guard outside, and your help has been boundless. For all this and much more we are grateful.

You will not find yourselves in these pages but you will find your names. Your Christian names and your surnames both seem so peculiarly Nova Scotian that we have borrowed them to help us hold, during these war years, the illusion at least of being less far apart.

FOG
MAGIC

BY JULIA L. SAUER

Published by
The Trumpet Club
1 Dag Hammarskjold Plaza
New York, New York 10017

Dell ® TM 681510, Dell Publishing Co., Inc.

RL: 5.0

ISBN: 0-440-84222-0

Reprinted by arrangement with Viking Penguin

Printed in the United States of America

October 1987

10 9 8 7 6 5 4 3

WFH

CONTENTS

FOG MAGIC

1. THE SPELL OF THE FOG

FROM the time she was a baby in her cradle, Greta had loved the fog.

Every soul in the little fishing village at the foot of the mountain had learned to accept the fog. It was part of their life. They knew that for weeks on end they must live within its circle. But they made no pretense of liking it. Those who tilled their little plots of land hated it when it kept their hay from drying. The men who fished dreaded it for it either kept them on shore altogether and cut down their meager earnings, or it made their hours on the sea more dangerous than ever. Only the lobster poachers who robbed honest men's lobster pots, or set their own out of season, liked it—the lobster poachers and small Greta. And with Greta it was more than liking. On days when the gray clouds of fog rolled in from the sea and spread over the village, she would watch it drift past the windows with a look on her small face that almost frightened her mother.

"Goodness, child," Gertrude Addington would say to the mite in the high chair, "you look as if you were seeing things—and pleasant things at that! I believe you like this beastly fog! Don't you know your father is out there, like as not running on a reef this very minute?

And my clean clothes mildewing for want of a bit of proper sun to dry them by?"

But then Greta would gurgle so happily and throw wide her arms with such eagerness to grasp and hold this queer gray smoke that Gertrude's irritability would vanish like the fog itself when the sun comes suddenly through.

As soon as Greta could walk, Gertrude found that she might as well put her housework aside on foggy days and give herself to minding her child. The first thin wraiths of fog in the high pasture were enough to set her small daughter's eyes sparkling. By the time it hid the big rock at the top of the pasture, Greta would be working her way cautiously to the door; and when it drew close enough to blur their own out-buildings, she would be scampering down the pasture lane as fast as her uncertain little feet could carry her.

"I'm at my wits' end minding the child on foggy days," she said to old Kil. He had stopped on his way home from the smoke house to leave a finnan haddie and he smiled down now at the bedraggled small girl whom Gertrude had just retrieved from beyond the garden. The old man laughed at her.

"Some are moon-struck, they say, and some are sun-struck," he said. "Maybe this one is fog-struck. Don't worry about her, Gertrude. It's good for a young one to want to know the world she lives in in all kinds of weather." He ran his big hand lightly over her damp curls. "I can't see that it does this little mess o' sea weed any harm to be well wetted down. But you might try mooring her to the apple tree and save yourself the minding of her."

So the small girl came to be moored at the end of the clothes line like an idle dory on every day when the gray wisps of fog came drifting in.

Greta was ten when she began to sense that she was looking for something within the fog. Until then it had only given her a happy feeling—just as the first snowflakes delighted some of the other girls and boys, or the first fall winds that set the birch leaves blowing. But from the day when she had gone alone to find old Rosie, the cow, nothing had been quite the same.

The village of Little Valley lay on a narrow neck of land between two great arms of the sea. Like a lazy giant, North Mountain lay sprawled the full length of the peninsula until, at the very end, it sat up in a startled precipice at the sight of the open sea. Years before, a number of villages had dotted the shore on either side. Now, only a few were left and those were dwindling in size as the men despaired of making a living by fishing. At the foot of the mountain and following the line of its base ran the highway. Here the Royal Mail, the grocery truck, the butcher, and the tourist who had lost his way made his daily or weekly or chance trip down the neck

to the sea and back again. But there was another road—
a road less direct—filled with convenient curves—the
old Post Road. This was the road the first settlers had
built in the wilderness. They had come by sea, many
of them, and made their little clearings near the shore.
Gradually they had extended their clearings inland and
in time, and with tremendous effort, they had threaded
their holdings together on a narrow uncertain road
through the spruce forest. With the new highway, gen-
erations later, had come new houses, away from the
shore and more sheltered. Only cellar holes remained
to mark the earlier homes.

This old Post Road was a joy to Greta. A part of it ran
through her father's land. Even though it had fallen
so low as to serve as a mere lane to the pastures, there
was something grand and romantic about it still. Years
of spring freshets had washed away the dirt. The stones
were bare that had formed its foundation. To follow it
was like walking in the bed of a dry mountain stream.
Greta knew every stone, every curve of it for miles, up
over the high pastures and then down again toward
the sea. This was the road her forefathers had traveled.
Surely, she thought, it must lead somewhere worth going.

And then there was the day when old Rosie was par-
ticularly stubborn.

"Greta! Greta!" her mother called her from play.

"Rosie isn't at the bars with the other cows. Your father's had a hard day getting in the hay. You'd best go and look for her before he does. You'll probably meet her on the way. You'll not need to go far."

Greta started willingly enough. She had heard the foghorn blowing at Tollerton, down in the Passage, and she knew there was fog on the way.

"Want me to go along?" one of the boys asked.

"You better not, Hazen. I may be late." She thanked him hastily and hurried away. To be caught in the fog and with the best excuse in the world was something too precious to share.

She found Rosie far off the Old Road and down at the cove. Rosie looked anything but guilty. Greta laughed.

"You darling," she said to her. "I think you stayed down here on purpose so I could drive you home in the fog. But that's not fair, you know, because Father would have had to come if Mother hadn't noticed."

She hurried Rosie across the stones of the shore and up through the thick spruce trees to the clearing beyond. The fog was closing in rapidly. You didn't notice it in the woods, but out in the open it was already thick. Even Rosie began to look soft and furry and indistinct, like an imaginary cow that you tried to see in the clouds.

It was just as they turned out of the path to the cove and into the Old Road that Greta happened to look off to the south.

"Rosie, wait," she called sharply.

She caught her breath and stared. If only stupid old Rosie could see it, too. Surely there was the outline of a building. It was blurred and indistinct, but those straight upright lines, that steep angle—no spruces could look *that* way. Greta's heart almost stopped beating, but she had no silly feeling of fear. Fog had always seemed to her like the magic spell in the old fairy tales— a spell that caught you up and kept you as safe, once you were inside it, as you would have been within a soap bubble. But this was stranger than anything she had ever seen before. Here was a house—a house where no house stood! Indistinct though it was, she could follow every line of it. A high sharp roof, a peaked gable, a little lean-to at the side. It was all there. Just such a house as those she saw every day in the village.

"So this," she said to herself, "*this* is what can happen to you in a fog. I always knew that there must be something hidden."

It was the most exciting thing that had ever happened to her in her whole life. Rosie, far ahead, was mooing at the pasture bars, and Greta tore herself away to follow. Once inside the barn, she wished that she had stayed and gone closer.

She stood in the barn doorway looking out across the yard. The fog was dense and gray. It blanketed the yard and made the house across the intervening feet as dim as that other one had been. Behind her in the quiet sweet-smelling barn her father sat milking.

"Father," Greta spoke softly.

"Yes? What is it, Greta?" The milk streamed rhythmically into the pail.

"Father, down where the path to Little Cove turns off the Old Road, is there—is there any old house off in the spruces to the south?"

Her father never stirred on the milking stool, but he dropped his hands quietly on his knees. The barn was very still for a moment.

"There's an old cellar hole off there, Greta," he said at last. "There's been no house upon it in my day." His voice was as calm and slow as ever. And then he added something very strange. "Every cellar hole should have a house," he said quietly.

"Yes, Father," Greta answered. It was almost as if he'd told her that *she* should build a house and she had almost promised.

Rosie stirred restlessly. Father cleared his throat and went on milking.

"You'd best go in and help your mother with the tea," he said. "She'll be fussing. She doesn't know you're back."

Greta stepped out of the warm fragrant barn into the

cool fog. It had always seemed to be whispering a secret to her. Now, at last, the words of the secret were coming more clearly.

Greta did not know what Walter Addington and his wife talked about that night. She went up to bed at her usual bedtime. Her little room with its steep sloping ceiling and its single window faced out toward the high pasture and the Old Road. Tonight you couldn't even see as far as the crooked apple tree by the well. She undressed and slipped into bed. The hushed voices in the room below and the distant rhythmic blowing of the foghorn in the Passage gave her the same warm, safe feeling they had always given her as she drifted off to sleep.

Whatever it was that was said that night, Gertrude was persuaded to let her child wander as she willed in the fog. Father had somehow worked the miracle. Sometimes Gertrude would look so perplexed, so distressed when Greta had finished her stint of housework and was free to go that the girl would come running back to throw her arms around her mother's neck.

"Why, Mother," she would say, "can't you see the fog is lovely? And I know every stone in the Old Road. I *can't* get lost. Please, *please* don't hate to let me go."

"Go on, child, go if you must." Gertrude would even laugh a little at her own vague fears. "It's just that you're so different from what *I* used to be at your age. We always hated this miserable wet fog. We'd scurry for home at the first sign of it." It was always the same. They never could understand each other about the fog.

One Saturday morning Greta opened her eyes to see a gray blanket filling the window space. A thick fog, and on a Saturday, too, when there was no school! It was the first really foggy day since the night she had seen the strange house back in the spruces—the first chance she had had to see if she had imagined it all. She hurried through her Saturday work. She thought of every little thing her mother could possibly want done—the usual Saturday errands, the washing up. Her own little room was as tidy as a ship's cabin, her Sunday gloves were washed and hung on the bars over the stove to dry. The collar was pressed on her best dress. Gertrude eyed her sharply.

"I know why you're so light on your feet this morning," she said shortly. "You're wanting to go off again."

Greta laughed. Not even her mother's crossness could spoil this day.

"I may go, mayn't I, Mother?" she coaxed. "It's only eleven o'clock, and if I take a sandwich and start now, I can be way over the high pasture before noontime. *Please,* Mother. I may even find some early berries. At least I'll take a pail."

Gertrude had been churning. She was pressing the little pats of butter with an acorn stamp. She laid the stamp down and looked at Greta without a word.

"Mother," the girl said slowly. "Please try just once more to understand."

Gertrude's "Well?" wasn't encouraging and Greta began hesitantly.

"You—you know the way a spider web looks on foggy days. Strings and strings of the tiniest pearls, all in a lovely pattern. Well, everything else is different, too, when—when once you're inside," she finished stumblingly.

"Inside?" asked Gertrude sharply. "Inside *what*, I'd like to know?"

"Oh, just inside the fog," Greta told her. It was no use. She could never get it into words. No one else could see how the fog always seemed to her like a magic wall. You stepped through and walked until your own familiar house was gone. And then, sometime, something strange and wonderful would happen. She was sure of it.

She made her sandwich quickly, and pulled on her old coat and beret.

"Leave the bread tins and the dinner dishes for me, Mother. I'll wash them when I get back," she said as she opened the door.

"Don't be late," was her mother's answer. Then, a

little more pleasantly, "I'll save a plate of chowder for your tea. You'll like as not be chilled through."

Greta gave her a loving little squeeze as she slipped out. The day had begun well, and the best part of it lay hidden ahead of her.

2. THE HOUSE AT THE FORK

"PLEASE let there be a house today on the old cellar hole," Greta kept saying to herself as she hurried along the Old Road. But how *could* there be? You could see things, perhaps, in the twilight that were never there at noon. That was it, of course. It was evening when she had gone after Rosie. Nothing like that could happen in the daytime. "*Maybe* there will be!" "There *can't* be." "*Maybe* there will be." "There *can't* be." Back and forth, back and forth the two thoughts went ticking in her mind. Her heart was beginning to thump in time to them.

"I'd better stop and get my breath at the sailors' graves," she thought. It was a spot where Father often stopped for a moment. Greta had never asked him why. On clear days the village looked its prettiest from there. But Greta thought it was Father's way of paying respect to the shipwrecked sailors who had been washed ashore in the cove years and years ago. Just where the fences met at the corner of the Ezra Knoll, they had buried them. There was nothing to show who they were or where they'd come from—nothing, now, to mark the graves except Father's care that that corner of the hay field was never mowed. Greta leaned on the fence and looked down at the unmowed corner.

"I hope they didn't come from a West Indies port," she thought. "They'd hate even to be buried here if they loved steady sunshine."

When she came to the path to Little Cove, Greta drew a long breath and looked over toward the clump of spruces. What she saw set her heart thumping. It was there! Again through the gray mist she could trace the darker outline of a house! For a moment she was tempted to push closer—to explore. Something held her back—and she was always glad that it had. Because the dim shadow of a house there at the fork became, through all the strange months that followed, a sort of magic beacon. When she could see it, she went on. When it wasn't there, she learned to turn back. It was always to be trusted. Disobey its message and there was a long walk, but nothing more. Only when its presence pointed the way was it wise to go full speed ahead.

To avoid temptation, Greta turned quickly into the right hand fork that led to the high pasture. She didn't look back until she came to the burned patch where the berries grew. There, standing in the middle of the road, just where she had stopped a moment before, was the blurred figure of a bent old man. Where had he come from and who was he? No one she knew; she was

sure of that, somehow. As she looked down at him, his
hand shot up in the friendly gesture that old people in
the village always used. Greta took off her beret and
waved to him. He seemed satisfied. He moved toward
the house and out of sight.

As she climbed on Greta realized suddenly that the
words "Old Man Himion" were going over and over in
her mind. "Where on earth did I ever hear of 'Old Man
Himion?'" she asked herself. "Why, of course. It was
Old Man Himion who had found the shipwrecked sailors in the cove!" She had heard that name from her
grandfather. "And that must be Old Man Himion's
house!" she thought. "The very house he had left when
he had gone down to the cove on that morning after the
big tempest so many years ago."

"I think I've seen Old Man Himion. And I think I
know his house. And this fog is really truly magic," she
sang as she started across the open pasture. The berries
were thick and she stopped to pick for a while. Her pail
was a good third full when she reached the other side
of the open space.

The higher she climbed, the thicker the fog grew.
Hurriedly, in great clouds it rolled over the top of the
mountain. Then, its hurry spent, it spread out leisurely
over the slopes below. Greta had to watch the ground
closely to find her way. The rough foundation stones
of the Old Road were the only guide. At the upper edge

of the pasture the road plunged into the thick spruce woods that covered the top. The trees seemed to hold the gray curtain back. Here the road was like a narrow dim tunnel; gray blanket above, wet green side walls, no sound but the sound of fog dripping from the spruces.

It was so very quiet in the spruces that Greta found herself picking her way cautiously as if she were afraid to turn a stone or make the slightest noise. Once she stopped to listen to the stillness. It was then that she heard the sound of trotting horses! Not the slow plod of oxen that she was used to, not the whir or rattle of a car on the highway, but the sharp rhythmic beat of horses' feet. They were coming toward her! And coming the way she had come! Occasionally she could hear a grating sound as the metal rim of a wheel glanced off a stone. She stepped to the side of the road. Who could possibly be driving on the Old Road? And where had such horses come from? Surely there were none in the village or in the town thirty miles away capable of holding that steady pace up the mountain. Greta was too excited to be frightened. She could only peer down along the dim road she had come and wait. Louder and louder came the clipped "trot, trot!" Around the bend in the road below they came into sight—two smartly groomed horses and a surrey driven by a woman dressed in gorgeous plum colored silk. She was like a picture out of a book. Greta stared in amazement as the carriage

came nearer. She hardly realized that the driver had noticed her when the horses were pulled up sharply and
expertly swung to the right to cramp the wheels of the
surrey.

"Come, come, child!" said a sharp, impatient voice.
"Don't stand there dreaming in the fog. Climb in if
you're going over the mountain." Greta climbed in. As
she settled into the seat beside the driver, there was a
billowing surge and rustle of taffeta, a flick of the whip
and the horses were off.

Greta clung to the side of the surrey and stole a
glance at her companion. Stiff and straight and elegant
she sat, her eyes on the winding road. But at each mo-
tion of her arms as she drove there was a swish of costly
silk. Greta was conscious of it above the sound of the
horses. Who had talked of silk so rich and elegant that it
sounded this way? She tried to remember. Oh, now she
knew. It was Earl Frosst—the one the children called
"The Early Frost." He had been telling old stories in
the kitchen one night when she was doing her home-
work. His grandmother had been born on the other side
of the mountain in the village of Blue Cove. It had been
a rich village once and its women had dressed as few
women in that part of the province had dressed. Early
had said, "When Blue Cove women came over the
mountain, it sounded like a three-master coming up
into the wind!" Well, surely this purple taffeta would

sound like the sails of a three-master. Greta let a little chuckle escape her. The woman looked down at her sharply.

"Few travel the road to Blue Cove afoot," she said. "Why are *you* going?"

"I like to walk in the fog," Greta told her.

"*Walk* in it, yes. But God help the men in boats on a day like this."

"But, but—as long as they can hear Tollerton blowing, they know where they are." Greta tried to defend the fog.

"Tollerton? Tollerton?" the woman looked puzzled.

"Yes, Tollerton—the foghorn in the Passage, I mean," Greta said.

"Well, it's time they had a foghorn in the Passage— with that treacherous current pulling between the Neck and the Islands. But you're talking nonsense, child. I never heard tell of one."

Greta caught her breath sharply and listened. They were on the side of the mountain toward the open sea and the wind was blowing out of the southwest. Tollerton should have sounded more distinctly here than at home. But *there was no sound of it*. She had passed beyond the reach of Tollerton's warning voice.

The woman was silent. Her driving took all her attention as the road wound down from the level plateau. Greta was too excited to speak. She knew somehow with certainty that when the road swung down toward the sea she would not find the familiar empty beach. She would find instead the once prosperous village of Blue Cove.

3. THE VILLAGE OVER THE MOUNTAIN

Two GIANT boulders stood where the old Post Road left the plateau and began to wind down toward the sea. The road had insisted on squeezing between them when it might just as easily have gone around. Greta had often traced the scorings on their inner surfaces, the straight lines that marked the years of travel. The rocks loomed ahead in the fog. It was exciting to think of dashing between them behind these brisk horses. She gripped the side of the surrey and leaned forward. The woman beside her gave a short laugh and reached for the whip.

"Never fear, child. We'll make it," she said. "They're the sentinels that guard Blue Cove. None passes but has a right there." She paused. "But *they* pass safely," she added.

"Have *I* a right there, do you think?" Somehow the question had to be asked. The woman turned to look down squarely into the girl's face.

"You've no cause to worry. You've the look of one that was always welcome there," she said curtly. Then the horses took all her attention. The boulders were upon them, dark shadows in the mist. The horses lunged through, then settled quietly again to a steadier pace.

Greta knew what this part of the mountain was like in clear weather. To the south of the road there was still unbroken forest—scarred here and there with burned patches, but otherwise dark, mysterious, treacherous, with unexpected chasms. Along the edge of the road to the north a high protective hedge of spruce and alder had been left, cut here and there with entrances. Beyond the hedge lay a clearing that sloped gently toward the sea. And dotting this clearing were cellar holes. Smooth little depressions they were; covered with the quick-springing growth of the pasture. It looked almost as if the homes of the departed inhabitants had sunk quietly into the earth.

Greta had often played in these cellar holes. It was fun to imagine where each house had stood, where the doorways had been, where the single street had led. Sometimes the shape of the depressions gave a clue; often a flat stone marked a doorstep. Once she had dug up a tiny spoon in a cellar hole. A salt spoon it was, with a strange name engraved on the handle. Her father said it was the name of a packet that had gone down off the Islands, years and years ago. The little salt spoon was one of her most treasured possessions, kept carefully hidden under the handkerchiefs in her dresser drawer.

Suddenly the woman pulled the team to a stop. They

were opposite one of the entrances to the clearing. "You'd best get out here," she said abruptly.

Greta climbed quickly over the wheel. In front of her an archway, hung with its curtain of fog, opened into the clearing. But did it lead into the familiar pasture? Or did it lead to something very different? For the first time in all her wandering in the fog she hesitated. She turned back toward the surrey for reassurance. The woman was smiling at her now, kindly, all her grimness gone.

"Go on," she said gently. "In the second house you'll find Retha Morrill. You two will pull well together."

She touched the horses with her whip. Greta watched the surrey disappear into the thicker mists below. Then, with a pounding heart, she stepped through the arch of spruces.

Her feet crunched on gravel. She was walking on a neat path. At her right loomed a big barn. Beyond she traced the outlines of a house—small, neat, gray-shingled,—and another, and another. A smell of wood smoke was in the air. Something brushed against her ankle. She looked down. A gray cat, the largest she had ever seen, was looking at her pleasantly.

"You beauty," Greta said to her and stooped to stroke the long hair. But it was one thing to greet a guest and quite another to be touched. Without loss of dignity, without haste, the gray cat was simply beyond reach.

But she was leading the way, her plume of a tail erect. Where the second neat path turned off toward a house the cat looked back to be sure that Greta was following. Suddenly a door banged. Around the side of the house and down the path a little girl came running. She stopped when she saw Greta and gathered the cat into her arms. The two girls stood looking at each other.

"I'm Retha Morrill," said the Blue Cove child slowly, "and I think that Princess must have brought you." She smiled and took Greta's hand. "I'm glad you've come. Let's—let's go in to Mother."

Greta could think of nothing to say. She could only smile back and follow. But she knew, and Retha knew, that as the woman had said, they would pull well together. At the doorway Retha dropped Princess on the wide stone before the steps.

"Please wait here," she said. "I'll find Mother."

Greta nodded. She still wasn't sure of her voice. She watched Princess curl into a graceful heap on the stone —gray stone, gray fur, gray mist, gray shingles, all softly blending and blurring before her eyes. She knew that stone well. It had strange markings on it. She had often traced them with her finger where it lay in the empty pasture beside her favorite cellar hole.

There was a brisk step inside the house and a tall woman stood in the doorway. "Come in, child, come in," she began. Then she stopped and looked long at her visitor. And Greta looked up at her. She had never seen such blue eyes in all her life before—nor such *seeing* eyes. They were eyes that would always see through and beyond—even through the close mist of the fog itself. The woman put out her hand and drew Greta inside before she spoke again. Her voice was a little unsteady but very gentle.

"You are from over the mountain," she said. "I can tell. And I'd know it even if this were the sunniest day in the year."

Greta didn't quite know what the words meant but she knew somehow in her heart that she and this strange woman would understand each other without words. In just the flash of a moment they had traveled the longest road in the world—the road that leads from eye to eye.

"I am Laura Morrill," Retha's mother continued quietly. "Retha shouldn't have left you standing outside—not such a welcome guest. Now turn toward the light and let me look at you. Humph! Yes. You *must* be an Addington. Would your name be Greta, now? Yes?" She laughed. "So I guessed it right the very first time! Well, you have the Addington look and the Addington eyes, and there's always a Greta among the Addingtons! Yes, and there's always a child among the Addingtons that loves the fog it was born to. You're that child, I take it, in your generation." Her laughing face grew sober and she gave Greta a long, steady look. Then she smiled again quickly and smoothed back Greta's hair with a quick stroke of her hand.

"It's the things you were born to that give you satisfaction in this world, Greta. Leastwise, that's what I think. And maybe the fog's one of them. Not happiness, mind! Satisfaction isn't always happiness by a long sight; then again, it isn't sorrow either. But the rocks and the spruces and the fogs of your own land are things that nourish you. You can always have them, no matter what else you find or what else you lose. Now run along and let Retha show you the village. You two must get acquainted."

"May I leave my pail here?" Greta asked her. "I picked quite a few berries for Mother, coming over."

"Of course you may," Laura Morrill told her. "But that reminds me! You must be hungry. We're through our dinner long since but I'll get you something. I dare say you left home early."

"I brought a sandwich to eat on the way," Greta told her. "Only there hasn't been time."

"Sit right down and eat it here, then. Retha, you fetch a glass of milk and I'll get you a piece of strawberry pie. Retha went berrying early this morning, too, and I made my first wild strawberry pie of the season."

After Greta had eaten she and Retha went out to explore the village. Its single street followed the curve of the shore line. There were houses on only one side, with patches of gardens behind white fences. Across the road in a narrow stretch of meadow, cows were grazing. Thick spruces hedged the meadow in at the lower side where there was a sharp drop, almost a precipice, to the shore. But the street was high enough so that Greta knew on a clear day you could look from the houses straight out to the open sea.

It was pleasant walking slowly up the street with Retha, but Greta couldn't find anything to say. To ask questions might break the spell. She might find herself back again in the empty clearing. And Retha knew that it would be impolite to question a stranger. They reached the end of the street before either spoke.

"There's our school, and there's our church," Retha said. She pointed out the little white building across the end of the street next to the neat church with its steeple.

"The shore curves in here, and there's another bay down there where you can find all sorts of things to play with. Our church is nice. Sometime maybe you'll be here on a Sunday so you can see it inside. There isn't any burying ground," she added. "It's all rock here and we can't have our own. When folks die they have to go over the mountain to be buried. Now let's go back to the Post Road and I'll show you the shore and the wharf and the fish houses and the stores."

In one of the door yards two very small children

were playing. As they came near Greta saw that there was a man seated on the ground, his back against the fence. One child tripped and sat down heavily, jolting out an indignant wail. The man reached out a long arm. He set the small thing on its feet again as you would set a ninepin, and gave it a comforting pat. The wail died suddenly and the man slumped back. Greta laughed.

"He must like children," she said, "or they must like him. Why, he didn't even have to speak to that one."

"Sss-h," Retha warned her. "He *can't* speak, but we —we don't quite know—for sure—whether he can hear."

Whether he heard or only felt their approaching footsteps, the man turned suddenly and looked up at them between the pickets. A lean, dark, strange, and foreign face. The eyes were piercing, searching. Greta found she was standing quite still, giving this strange man a chance to look at her. Retha didn't seem to think it unusual. She was smiling at him and saying slowly,

"Anthony, this is my friend Greta Addington. She's from over the mountain." Then she pulled Greta gently away. The man turned to watch until they faded into the fog.

"But, Retha, you said he couldn't *hear*, and then you *spoke* to him. And he looks almost—almost savage. And still he was minding those babies."

"I said we don't *know* whether he hears or not. Or

whether he could speak if he wanted to. But he's not savage. He only looks that way when he sees a stranger. I guess it's because he's always trying to find someone —someone he knows, I mean. But, Greta, did you see his—his legs?"

"I didn't see anything but his eyes. And anyhow, he was almost hidden in that clump of monkshood. What about his legs?"

"He—he hasn't any," Retha said quietly.

"Hasn't any *legs?*" Greta could only stare in horror.

"They are gone just above his knees, so all he can do is crawl, and mind babies. But no matter how fierce he looks, *they* understand him. And he's always gentle."

"But what happened?"

Retha hesitated a moment. "We don't talk about him much. I'd like to ask Mother first if I should tell you. Let's go down to the wharf now." And Greta had to be content.

When they reached the Post Road, Retha pointed toward the shore. "See! The fog's lifting a little. You can see the end of the wharf from here and you couldn't see anything an hour ago. Come on."

Greta stood still. She couldn't explain it even to herself, but suddenly she knew how Cinderella felt when the first stroke of midnight began to sound.

"I think there isn't time to go down today, Retha," she said. "But I'd like to go next time I come. I must go home now. It'll be late when I get over the mountain."

"Your berries! You left your pail at our house," Retha reminded her.

They ran back to the house. In the doorway Mrs. Morrill stood holding the pail.

"The fog's lifting," she said quietly and held out the pail. "I put a piece of strawberry pie on top of your berries, but I don't think it'll crush them any. And come again, child. We'd like to see you often; that is, if your mother doesn't worry. You're like a visitor from another world." Then she added as an afterthought, "Coming as you do from over the mountain."

Greta thanked her and took the pail. Retha went as far as the Post Road with her. They said good-by hurriedly. Greta left without daring to turn back and wave.

It was almost clear when she reached home, but late. Her mother greeted her with relief. Father had finished milking and sat reading the paper. Greta's conscience hurt her. She hadn't once thought of the mail and someone else had gone to the post office. She held out the pail to her mother.

"There's a surprise in it, Mother," she said. Gertrude opened the pail.

"I *am* surprised," she said. "I never dreamed you'd find so many. It's early yet for strawberries."

Greta stood very still. Then she stepped over and

looked into the pail. There were the berries she had picked. *But there was nothing else in the pail!*

Suddenly she wanted to cry, but her father was looking at her over the top of his paper. He was smiling at her just with his eyes, but he looked as if he understood.

"Fog thick at Blue Cove today?" he asked.

"Heavens, child, have you been way over there?" asked her mother.

How did Father know she had been to Blue Cove? Greta no longer wanted to cry. She could look back at Father and almost smile.

"Yes, Father," she said. "It was very thick today."

"I thought so," he answered and went back to his paper.

4. THE SALVAGED EGG CUPS

THE WEATHER was clear until the close of school in June. Only once or twice, and then during the evening, could the people of Little Valley hear the fog-horn down in the Passage blowing its steady warning to vessels at sea.

During the last week of school, their teacher asked the children to vote on the place for their school picnic. Greta was as surprised as anyone to hear herself suggesting T. R.'s beach, "because they could swim there." T. R.'s beach lay on their own side of the mountain and Hazen turned around with astonished eyes.

"I never knew *you* to want to go anywhere but to Blue Cove," he whispered.

"Oh, *no!* Blue Cove! Blue Cove!" two or three others shouted before she could answer. "It's too cold for swimming, anyhow, and at Blue Cove we can play games in the clearing."

Mrs. Collins rapped on her desk. "We'll vote by raising our hands," she said. "Now, for T. R.'s beach?"

Greta, with Hazen loyally supporting her, raised her hand.

"Two. And now, for Blue Cove?" Every other hand in the room shot up. So it was settled; the picnic would be at Blue Cove. Greta could only hope for sunshine. "What if there's fog?" she thought. "Will I have to share the village with them? or won't it ever be there again—even for me—if we all go?" She needn't have worried. It was a clear day. There was no mystery, no strangeness, and when they trooped back over the mountain, Greta for the moment almost forgot that Blue Cove still had a secret life of its own.

The clear weather lasted well into July, and then one morning she woke to the steady sound of the Tollerton foghorn. The fog had swept in, blanketing everything. Even before she opened her eyes, Greta was conscious of the strange feeling of excitement that was beginning to mean fog to her. She hurried into her clothes, helped with the morning work, and then: "Mind if I go for a walk, Mother?" she asked casually.

"Go along," her mother said. "I've been expecting you'd want to." She set the kettle down hard in her irritation. "You'd best take a sandwich," she added. "The fresh bread will taste good with some of the sweet butter and jam."

"I think I won't bother with lunch, Mother." Greta was pulling on her beret.

"Why not?" There was suspicion in Gertrude's voice. "It only wants an hour and a half 'til dinner. You'll never be back by then."

Greta went into the buttery and cut two generous

slices of the soft brown oat bread. She couldn't explain how sure she was that Mrs. Morrill would ask her to dinner.

At the fork Greta stopped and peered into the spruces. Good! She could just make out the dim outlines of a house. She hurried on over the rough stones, across the high pasture and into the woods, sure and confident. Suddenly she realized that Tollerton was silent and she almost laughed out loud. She had crossed the line, as invisible as the equator, to another world.

Retha sat waiting for her, perched high on one of the Sentinel Rocks. "I was afraid you wouldn't be able to come so soon again," she began.

"But it's been *weeks!*" Greta replied.

"I know," Retha interrupted. "It's seemed like weeks to me, too, since yesterday. But that's just because I like you so much. And I guess because I've wanted someone my own age for so long. Sometimes I think it would be fun to live in a bigger village than ours. Here the boys go fishing or off in the vessels as soon as they're as old as I am. And all the girls are older than I am, or just babies. But now that you're here it will be easier to wait!"

"To wait for what?"

"Why, for Father, and the other men, to come home. There's a vessel aground. Didn't you know? I thought everybody on the Neck would have heard."

Greta shook her head. "We hadn't heard where I live," she said. "Where is she? Off shore here?"

"No, she's down off the Islands. She went aground yesterday on a ledge with a hole stove in her. Father's been gone since last night. Some of the men have come home to unload and gone back again."

"And the people on her? Are they safe?"

Retha nodded. "She's been given up for lost and they've taken off the crew and passengers, so now anyone who wants to, can go aboard her and take things. That's why Father's gone."

They had reached Retha's house. Mrs. Morrill stood in the doorway peering out into the fog. She looked worried, but smiled as she welcomed Greta.

"You'll find us all upset today, I expect," she said. "I hate salvage, myself, even if it *is* honest to take for yourselves what would only go to the bottom of the sea if you didn't. But run down to the shore, Retha, and take Greta. I thought I heard a boat come in. It may be your father."

At the foot of the steep road there was nothing as Greta knew it. A general store stood at the end of the road, with two little shops across from it. Below the cliff the wide beach was teeming with life. Fish houses and drying racks crowded each other for space under the bank; sheds and warehouses lined both sides of a road that led along the beach to a cluster of wharves. Oxen drawing a two-wheeled cart plodded up from the wharf. Through an open door Greta caught sight of a forge, with flames leaping in the dark and shadows creeping up the walls. But Retha gave her no time to watch. She led the way out onto the wharf and threw herself down flat to look over the edge. The tide was low and the small boat that had just come in was at the end of the slip.

"It isn't Father," Retha said in disappointment. "It's Reg Frosst's boat. But like as not he'll know something about Father. What do you suppose they've got?"

The men below were lifting out bundles tied in blankets. Some they had tossed onto the ways; others they set down with the greatest care.

"What *can* that long box be, Retha? It's as long as a coffin but it's too narrow."

"I don't know," Retha answered. "Maybe it's just a case that something's packed in." At that moment there was a br-r-r, and slow measured tones came from the box —one, two, three, up to twelve. A shout went up from the men.

"Never missed a beat, not even for a shipwreck," one said.

"Here's a sea-going clock for you, Reg," laughed another. "Seems a pity, now, she should have to end her days ashore."

"Her life *began* ashore, in some old captain's front

hall, I'll be bound. So she may as well end it ashore," said the man named Reg. "But some day maybe I'll have a vessel of my own with a cabin big enough for her. And if I do, I'll take her to sea again. But easy there, Sid, I aim to show her to Martha in one piece."

As they started up the sloping ways, Retha called down to Reg, "Have you seen my father? Has he started back?"

"He started when we did, Retha," Reg told her, "but he put in at Gull Cove with a set of instruments for old Doc Ingraham. The doctor that left 'em behind must a been mighty rattled, because they were as bright and shiny as a well-trimmed lamp."

Retha and Greta watched the slow procession up the wharf. Helpers had appeared from all directions. The smith came running, small boys slid dangerously underfoot on the long ways, green with the seaweed that the low tide exposed. With good-natured joking the long case was carried up to the beach and out of sight along the road to the houses above. A sharp cry floated down from the cliff followed by the reassuring laughter of the men. Some woman had run out of her house and caught a glimpse of the long dark case that looked so like a stretcher.

The girls turned to the open sea again. The dense wall of fog hung like a curtain just beyond the edge of the wharf, but through it came the muffled sound of a boat. A moment later another small boat nosed cautiously into the slip.

"Father! It's Father!" Retha pulled Greta to her feet. They ran back along the wharf to the top of the ways and started down the wet planking. Near the bottom Greta lost her footing and shot helplessly toward the water. Eldred Morrill caught her belt, swung her to her feet and steadied her.

"It's Greta, Father. I told you about her. She's from over the mountain."

The tall man looked at her long and seriously. The other men in the boat stared curiously, too.

"So you're Greta from over the mountain," he said at last. "Retha and my wife could talk of nothing else last night. Come often, child. We're glad to have you. But be careful while you're here. If anything happened to you—" there was a long pause, "—we wouldn't have any way of explaining to your folks," he finished at last. And then: "Can you girls carry some bundles? I've brought your mother some blankets. She can always use more."

He loaded light bundles into their arms and watched until they were safely on solid ground. Then he and his companions sorted their salvage and followed.

Mrs. Morrill was waiting for them at the gate. At other gates along the single street, other women, whose husbands and sons had not returned, stood peering into the fog. For some of them Mr. Morrill had a word or a message. The others turned away in disappointment. Inside, Mrs. Morrill hurried about getting some food onto the table, and called Retha to help.

"Oh, come, Laura," said Mr. Morrill. "Don't you even want to see what I brought you? I found something very special for my girls—and something *small*. Retha always likes a *small* package best."

Mrs. Morrill came, wiping her hands on her apron, and Retha strangled her father with a hug. From an inner pocket he pulled out two little silver egg cups, two tiny silver egg spoons and two still smaller spoons.

"Oh, Father, what *darling* little things!" Retha cried. "And real silver. Why, this littlest spoon must belong to a doll's set. Father, I *love* them, they're so little."

"Well, they may not be *real* silver," Eldred Morrill told her. "Even a grand packet like this wouldn't have real silver—unless they belonged to the captain's mess. And I doubt that there were any dolls aboard. The little spoons are salt spoons, I reckon."

"I don't care if they are. My doll is going to have mine for her porridge."

Mrs. Morrill was smiling down at the tiny spoons that Father had laid in her hand. "I'm glad you brought me blankets," she said. "They are so much lighter to sleep under than quilts. And Greta shall have my egg cup and the little spoons to remember this day by."

She held them out to her. Greta took them, hardly able to stammer her thanks.

"Oh, Mother, how nice!" said Retha. "Now when I'm eating my egg I'll know that Greta is using an egg cup just like it."

Greta thought of the strawberry pie and she looked up hastily, a question in her eyes, in time to see Mr. and Mrs. Morrill exchange a look. There was silence for a minute. Even Princess stopped washing herself and looked up. Mrs. Morrill spoke very quietly at last.

"They'll always be *yours,* Greta, to remember a beautiful ship by that went down at sea. But we hope you'll be coming over the mountain often. Couldn't you enjoy them just as much if you left them here? And used them whenever you came? I'll cook an egg right now for each of you," she finished more briskly.

"I guess maybe that would be better, Mrs. Morrill, and thank you," said Greta.

"Goody," said Retha, "then I'll know you are always coming back. And, Mother, may we keep them here in the very center of the corner cupboard? See, Greta, this can be the place of honor, here in front of this dinner plate. This is awfully precious, too. It came up once in Grandfather Tidd's net without a chip out of it. But I'll never use mine unless you are here too."

"Wash them now, girls," Laura Morrill said. "Your eggs are ready to come out. It's a queer dinner that begins with an egg. But it's a queer meal, anyway, at this time of day."

At dinner they heard more of the wreck. The vessel was gone. It had slipped clean off the ledge when the tide turned.

"We had almost no warning," Eldred Morrill said. "Luckily, there were only a few boats moored to her at the time. Yesterday there were dozens. If she had gone then there isn't a house on the Neck today that wouldn't be grieving for at least one man. She would have taken them all with her to the bottom. But the men near by, who'd got there first, were well-nigh worn out lugging their salvage ashore. And most of them were sleeping. Only a few of us from up the Neck were aboard. I don't know what it was—exactly—that warned me; a whisper of wind, maybe, or a quiver or something. But all at once I knew I wanted to go—and to go quick. I picked up the blankets and rushed to port. Howe and Don and Earl all came hurrying. Nobody spoke. We climbed down into the dories, and the others came swarming over the rail. Some of them even cut their lines instead of untying them. Every one of us was as sure he'd had a warning as if he'd felt the hand of the Lord Himself on his shoulder. We pulled off as fast as we could go, but we slowed down where we could just see her through the fog and waited. It wasn't long. There was another little breath of wind, like a sigh, almost. The fog opened up a mite and we could see her plain for a minute. And then she slipped out of sight. I never saw anything like it—except a lazy whale turning over, maybe. Even the backwash was different than usual—just one great slow wave. Howe had pulled off his hat, and the rest of us did, too. It's hard to see a good vessel go down even if she doesn't take anyone with her."

"Anyhow we'll always remember her," Greta broke the silence by saying. "I'm glad her name is on the egg cup and even on the littlest spoons."

"And it's on your blankets, too, Mother," Retha discovered. "See, here on the corner of each one. But blankets will wear out and our egg cups and spoons will last forever and forever."

The afternoon was well along before the dishes were washed and put away. Mr. Morrill started down to the shore but came back again. He fumbled on the clock shelf until Mrs. Morrill asked him if he had lost something.

"No," he answered slowly, "but I think we'll have a pleasant evening. The wind's changing and the fog's beginning to lift." Then he went out again.

Greta hung the dish towel she had been using neatly on the bar over the stove. "Maybe I had better start home," she said.

"Perhaps you had, Greta," said Mrs. Morrill quietly. She shook her head at Retha's protest. "We must never coax Greta to stay," she went on firmly, "but we hope she will come soon again."

Retha went up the road with her as far as the Sentinel Rocks. They said good-by and Greta went on alone over the mountain toward home.

5. LOST ANN

RASPBERRIES were ripe. Wild and sweet, they grew bountifully in all the burned patches on the mountain but none were so large as those in a certain clearing just off the Old Road near the deserted village. The children of Little Valley had planned an all-day berrying trip over the mountain but when the day came it was one blanketed in fog. They gathered on the unroofed side stoop at Greta's to talk it over.

"Oh, it'll burn off by noon," Hazen said. One or two of the other boys who had brought their lard pails and sandwiches agreed with him. But the girls were doubtful. Where the Old Road led through the spruce woods it would be dismal and wet, with moisture dripping from every bough. It wouldn't be half the fun to go on such a day, they thought.

"The berries will keep another day," said Frieda. "They won't even ripen much on a day like this." Greta had little to say, but when they finally decided not to go and scattered in disappointment to their homes she wasn't sorry. She watched them out of sight and then hurried indoors to pull on her old sweater and beret. It was just the right sort of day to go over the mountain alone.

At Blue Cove she met Retha coming out of her house, carrying a pail. "I'll get you a pail, too," Retha said. "But maybe you'd rather just come along. I'll love having you—and you needn't work," she added.

"Of course I want to pick," Greta told her.

They went back for another pail and Mrs. Morrill hastily buttered some extra slices of bread.

In the clearing some women and older girls were already at work. They picked quietly, with little conversation. It was serious work—this gathering of the few fruits that would mean so much in the winter when fish and potatoes, and bread and tea were often their monotonous diet for long weeks. Retha and Greta were subdued by the industry around them. They edged their way over to one side where they felt free to talk while they worked. By noon the big pails were two-thirds full. The earlier comers had left and the clearing was deserted.

"Can't we eat now?" said Greta. "I can't bear the smell of your mother's bread for another minute."

Retha laughed. "I'm starved, too. Let's leave our pails here and go into the woods. I know a flat rock where we can eat. It's not very far."

They pushed into the spruces and followed a little path along the edge of a gulch until they came to Retha's flat rock. It was dry and warm. They spread their napkins out and piled the slices of oat bread on them. When the last crumb was gone, they stretched out and lay quietly for a few minutes. The fog had been sucked upward by the draft leaving the spot where they lay clear. All around them were trees shrouded with gray wisps of fog. The sounds that came to them were muffled. Overhead, close but out of sight, there was the creaking sound of a gull in flight; near by, soft twitterings, the rustlings of small creatures, and the constant drip of moisture from the trees.

Retha gave a contented little sigh. "I love it here," she said. "I think this is my favorite rock. I know that really we aren't ten minutes from home. But I like to pretend we are all alone in the wilderness."

Greta was too comfortable to reply. She had turned over on her stomach. With her chin resting on her crossed arms she could look along the ground beneath the low branches toward other light spots where other flat rocks made oases in the woods. Suddenly she was aware that they were *not* alone in the wilderness. *She was looking straight into the face of another girl!* She, too, was stretched out on a rock. She was older than they, her long hair was in braids and her face was white and frightened. Without taking her eyes from the other girl, Greta pulled Retha toward her. "Look—there," she whispered.

It took Retha a moment to find the still figure staring at them. Then she sprang to her feet calling, "Ann, Ann!

Wait!" She plunged into the woods toward the strange girl. Greta followed as fast as she could, but Retha seemed desperate in her haste. When she caught up with her, Retha was kneeling on the flat rock and sobbing.

"See, she's been lying right here. The moss is all crushed. She can't be far. We've *got* to find her. Come on."

"Why have we?" Greta wanted to know, but Retha didn't answer.

She plunged into the woods again, calling over and over, "Ann! *Wait,* I tell you. I'm Retha Morrill. You don't *need* to run. *Wait* for me."

It seemed hours to Greta that she crashed through the woods trying to keep up with Retha. They scrambled through places she would have thought impenetrable. Their clothes caught on dead limbs, she slipped down into gulches and climbed out again. It was frightening to have quiet Retha so excited, and the thought of being left behind on a strange part of the mountain was terrifying, too. They went on and on through the dim woods. Twice they caught a glimpse of the tall, thin girl they were pursuing. She would stand and rest and then vanish like a deer. At last, when she was too exhausted to go farther, Retha threw herself down and sobbed helplessly. Greta put a protecting arm around her. There was nothing she could do but wait. As soon as Retha was quieter, she said to her, "We've got to get home, Retha. Whoever she is, we'll never catch up with her. And it's late. And I don't know the way back."

Retha sat up and looked around. "I do," she said miserably. "We'd best follow the gulch to the shore and climb back along the rocks."

They were weary when they finally dragged themselves up the road from the beach and into the Morrill's cheerful kitchen. Mrs. Morrill looked at them in surprise. "Why, girls—" she began. But Retha interrupted.

"Mother, we've seen Ann. She *hasn't* run away to friends somewhere, like people think. She's still out there in the woods. And she looks terrible—and—and hungry."

"Are you sure? And did you tell her the money's been found? That she has no cause to run away? Did you see her, too, Greta?"

Greta nodded. "But we couldn't tell her anything. We couldn't get close enough," she added.

Mr. Morrill came in.

"The girls think they've seen Ann in the woods," Mrs. Morrill told him. There was pity and anxiety in her voice. "Could she have kept herself alive all this time do you think?"

"She might," Eldred Morrill admitted. "On strawberries and now the raspberries. But I don't see how!"

"But she *has*. We *saw* her," Retha insisted.

"I'll get the men and we'll go out again and search," Mr. Morrill promised. "Tell me exactly where you were when you saw her first and which way she went." They told him as well as they could.

"Does Greta know what this is all about?" he asked. Greta shook her head.

"Ann lived down below here on the Neck," Mrs. Morrill told her. As she talked, she began putting up a bite of lunch for Mr. Morrill to take along. "She worked for a hard sort of man. She hadn't any kin folks of her own and she was a frightened young one—always. The man she worked for had been saving for a year to buy a yoke of oxen. He kept this money in a tin box hidden in his house—it wasn't much more than a shack, anyhow. One day—early in the spring it was—the box was gone. He accused Ann of taking it. The girl ran out of the house, so they say, just as she was—no coat, even, to keep her warm. Two days later he found his money —the box had slipped down behind the studding where he'd hid it. Well, they searched for Ann for two weeks. The men, even up here, went out in parties day after day. But they never found her. And we've kind of stopped worrying. Most folks thought she'd gone up the valley and found work somewhere. Some *do* say they'd seen her in the woods, but the rest of us didn't take much stock in it." She stopped suddenly. "Why, Greta!

What's the matter, child? You're white as a sheet! I know it's not a pleasant story, but no real harm can come to the girl—even if she does run wild for a spell."

"But *I've* heard people talk of Ann," Greta's lips were trembling. "They'd say 'Be careful you don't meet Ann in the woods' and things like that. And my father said they meant the ghost of a girl who had been unjustly accused and who still haunts the woods."

Mr. Morrill smiled. "We'll see that this Ann doesn't haunt the woods," he said. But Greta was terribly in earnest.

"But Mr. Morrill," she insisted, "Father says that years later they found Ann's skeleton up near the bottomless lake!"

Mr. and Mrs. Morrill looked at each other. There was dismay on both their faces. Mr. Morrill reached for his coat and lantern hurriedly.

"Don't worry," he said. "We'll find this Ann all right. But she's a *stupid* young one all the same. If *we* all know she's innocent, *she* must know it," he added with exasperation. "And there's no sense in running away."

Mrs. Morrill put a comforting arm around Greta. "It's late, Greta. I'm sorry we can't keep you because I know you're tired. But you'd best go. Are you sure you're not afraid to go over the mountain alone? Someone could go with you." She hesitated for a moment and then added, "At least as far as the Sentinel Rocks."

Greta shook her head and said good-by. But she hurried more than usual that night, and where the Old Road led through the spruces she stopped for a minute to call softly into the dark shadows, "Ann! Ann, come back. They *know* you are innocent." There was no answer and she ran toward the lights of Little Valley with thankfulness for her safe, welcoming home.

6. *TO HALIFAX FOR JUSTICE*

As the village of Blue Cove grew more and more real to Greta, she learned to fit it into her own life. It was easier even than having faith. The Bible taught that "faith is the substance of things hoped for, the evidence of things not seen." But Blue Cove with its winding street of houses above the cliff, its busy beach and wharves below, was something Greta believed she saw with her own eyes. Perhaps, if only she could keep it secret enough, she could go on seeing it always. She would have liked to talk to Retha about it and about themselves. She even tried once, but Retha stopped her.

"I know, Greta," she said softly, "I tried to ask Mother about us once, too."

"What did she say?" Greta asked her.

Retha thought for a minute. Then she said slowly, "She didn't really answer. Maybe she was thinking about something else because all she said was 'that women who stay ashore have to learn the same lesson that men learn who go to sea.'"

"*What* lesson? Did you ask her that?"

"Yes. And she said 'they have to learn to be content and at peace shut in by their horizon.'"

Greta was turning the words over in her mind one

day as she hurried along the Old Road. Her mother had decided it was too foggy for a wash day and she was unexpectedly free to go off by herself. She waved to Old Man Himion absent-mindedly as she passed the fork and started up the mountain. "To learn to be content and at peace shut in by their horizon," she repeated. Suddenly it was all clear to her.

"When I'm inside, it's the fog that is my horizon," she thought. "And all I need to do is to be content." It was answer enough for a happy little girl on her way to adventure.

Her happiness was subdued somewhat when she found the Morrills bustling around to get ready for church. You could never tell, Greta had learned long before, on what day of the week you would arrive at Blue Cove. The seasons could be depended on. If the blueberries were ripening in Little Valley, they would be ripening in Blue Cove. But like as not a Tuesday in one place would be a Thursday in the other.

Greta felt a little shy about going to church, but the moment she was settled in the pew between Retha and her mother, all feeling of strangeness passed. The words of the Gospel and the familiar hymns could smooth away years or centuries.

Today Greta was not the only stranger in church. In a front pew, with the woman who had given her a ride over the mountain, sat a tall, stately woman.

Beside the rich silk of her companion she seemed to be plainly dressed, but there was something about the proud way in which she held her head that made Greta long to see her face.

"It's Mrs. Stanton from down off the Islands," Retha whispered. "That is Mrs. Trask she is with, and they're both coming to our house to dinner."

When the service was finally over and the congregation rustled out into the aisle, Greta watched for the stranger to turn. The face that she saw was not old, but it was worn and tired. It was a face you remembered.

Mrs. Morrill had taken it for granted that Greta was to stay for dinner in spite of the expected guests, and Retha had set an extra place next to her own. The Morrills' table looked as Greta had never seen it before. It was set with blue willow dishes that Grandfather Morrill had brought home from a voyage. There was a bouquet of swamp orchids and meadow-rue in an old ginger jar, and at each place a tiny dish of baked-apple —that most precious of all preserves—made vivid spots of gold up and down the table.

All through dinner, Greta found herself watching Mrs. Stanton. She had been beautiful once and would be again, she decided, if only she could look less troubled.

Mrs. Trask seemed glad to see Greta. She tilted up her chin and pushed a lock of hair behind her ear as she said brusquely, "So it's the fog-struck young one again! Well, I was right, wasn't I, when I said you and Retha would pull well together?" That was all, but there was kindness behind the harsh voice and Greta liked her.

When the dinner work was done, the girls slipped into the best room where the women sat waiting for Mrs. Morrill, and those who had helped her, to join them. Others had come since dinner and they settled themselves to polite conversation, but Mrs. Trask interrupted it.

"Ardis Stanton," she said with a short laugh, "there's no sense in pretending we aren't wondering why you're here, and our curiosity is like to kill us. We all grew up together and we went to your wedding. But we've scarce seen you since Aubry Stanton took you to live down on the Island. And now you come back afoot to visit, with no luggage but a parcel. What's amiss, Ardis? We're your friends," she ended more gently.

Mrs. Stanton sat very erect in her chair before she began to speak. "I've come upon evil days," she said finally. "When Aubry was lost at sea, he left me well off. We owned near a third of the Island, and good land most of it was, too. And we owned it *fair*. It had come to him straight from his father and he'd had it from *his* father. The first Stantons had claimed it by right of settlement over sixty years ago."

"And what's happened, Ardis? You've not had to sell, have you?" Mrs. Morrill asked.

"No," said Mrs. Stanton and her face grew more bitter. "No, I've not had to sell. I was managing right well, though I'll admit it was hard going some of the time. Five children, and the youngest not born when his father was lost . . ." She stopped as if she were reviewing the hard years over again. Mrs. Trask's impatient voice brought her back.

"Well, something worse than that has happened to you—I can tell," she said. "You're not one to grieve overlong at hard work—unless you've changed since you left home."

"Worse things *have* happened to me," Mrs. Stanton said quietly. "A man has come—claiming every acre of our land. He says he has a grant to it from the Crown. I've been five years trying to get justice. I've written to every official here and abroad I can think of. I've used up every bit of gold I had saved. I've sent my jewelry to pay for an agent in London to get my rights. It's all gone and—and nothing happens. He threatens to turn us out. And I'm afraid he can do it," she finished.

There were murmurs of sympathy from the women. Even Mrs. Trask was at a loss, but she recovered herself first. "And what do you aim to do *now?*" she questioned.

"I'm going to walk to Halifax to get justice," said Mrs. Stanton.

"Walk? To Halifax?" The women were incredulous.

"Why not?" asked Mrs. Stanton. "I've no money for coach fare even where there are coaches to ride in."

"Ardis Stanton, that's false pride," Mrs. Morrill began. "You know we'd like to——"

The expression on Mrs. Stanton's face stopped her. "I know you would," she said. "And I'll take food and a night's lodging from my friends in gratitude. I'll take a lift on my way, if anyone's going. The neighbors have taken the children to care for while I'm gone, but that's something I can repay. Aside from that I'll take no help, neither for myself nor for my children. Maybe you can't understand until you've been through something like this yourselves. But a time comes when it seems that no help and no kindness will serve—there's something *gnawing* at you that only justice will satisfy."

"But, Ardis, how do you aim to *get* justice? All alone, by yourself, in Halifax?"

"I aim to see the young Duke of Kent, myself. Maybe, since *he* came out to the province, things'll be different in Halifax."

Greta had been listening so intently to the conversation that she spoke without thinking. "It was the Duke of Kent who married the Princess Marina, wasn't it? I've seen their pictures!"

The ladies turned startled eyes on her. Then a polite

little titter swept over the room. Mrs. Trask recovered first.

"I'm afraid, my dear," she said, "I'm afraid, from what we hear, that the Duke of Kent is hardly a *marrying* man." Another laugh followed which Greta didn't understand. She was glad when they forgot her again and the conversation continued.

"You'll have a difficult time getting to see the Duke, Ardis, unless you have powerful friends in Halifax," someone remarked.

"I dare say I will," Mrs. Stanton agreed. "But I have a plan in mind. I can only try and pray the Lord it works."

Old Mrs. Morehouse spoke for the first time. She had been sitting by the window in the little straight-backed Loyalist rocker that had come from Massachusetts. In the gray light that filtered in through the fog, her beautiful face glowed like a moonstone. "What are you carrying in your package, Ardis?" she asked gently.

"My wedding dress and my great-grandmother's earrings," Mrs. Stanton replied. "They're all I have left."

"You were a beautiful bride, Ardis Stanton," Mrs. Morehouse told her. "I can't remember a lovelier one. I think you'll succeed, my dear," she added after a pause, "because you deserve to. We'll all pray for your success."

Mrs. Trask spoke up sharply to hide the fact that even she was sniffing into her handkerchief.

"I'm driving up the valley myself tomorrow, Ardis,"

she said. "I'll take you a piece on your way and no trouble at all."

The room seemed to be growing lighter and Greta went to the window to look out. The wind must have shifted because the late afternoon sunshine was glowing through the fog.

"I must go," she whispered to Retha. Mrs. Morrill nodded to her across the room and she seemed relieved that Greta had noticed the weather.

All the next morning Greta watched the old Post Road. An ox team lumbered down, hauling a load of stone from the high pasture. But no surrey came down drawn by two smart horses. She told herself that she hadn't really expected to see one.

58 ANTHONY

r own home lacked. But then there were

7. *ANTHONY*

WHEN school opened in September, Greta had les
and less time to think of Blue Cove. But it wa
never quite out of her mind. Most of us live in twe
worlds—our real world and the one we build or spir
for ourselves out of the books we read, the heroes we
admire, the things we hope to do. Greta's other world
was Blue Cove. She played no part in it except as a
visitor. Its life went on without her. Still, each time a
fog closed in and she stepped into it, out of sight of her
everyday life, she felt as drawn to the secret village over
the mountain as if the turn of the tide down in Petit
Passage had caught her up with its smooth power.

Sometimes on her visits she would do nothing but sit
in Mrs. Morrill's kitchen and watch her weave, content
just to be there and hold Princess. Mrs. Morrill had begun work on one of the first woven carpets in the province. It was to cover her entire parlor floor. The hooked
mats would do well enough for the kitchen and the
bedrooms, she said. Greta wished that they used more
hooked mats at home instead of exchanging them always
for the congoleum squares and strips that were so easy
to keep clean. Hooked mats suited the house better, she
thought. They gave Mrs. Morrill's cheerful kitchen a

richness her own home lacked. But then there were many things about the Blue Cove houses that interested Greta, though outwardly the houses were just the same. But Blue Cove menfolk all went to sea at some time or other in their lives. Their vessels plied back and forth to the West Indies at least, and if they didn't go to the Far East themselves, they often bespoke vessels that did. There were many chances to bring back curios and china, and the silks that made their womenfolk rustle "like a three-master coming up into the wind." Greta laughed each time she thought of Early Frosst's description. All these things that they had brought back still graced their houses; married sons and daughters and grandchildren had not yet coaxed them from their elders and carried them away to their own distant homes.

On one such quiet afternoon, Mrs. Morrill was telling the girls about the time the whole village had nearly been wiped out at once. They had gone across the bay on Captain Landers's vessel to a cherry festival. The vessel had turned over in a sudden squall. But they had clung to it until help came and not a soul aboard was lost, except one small dog asleep in the cabin. Mrs. Morrill was interrupted by the sound of voices coming up from the shore.

"Run out, girls," she said, "and see what's happened. It sounds as if every man and child in town was coming up the road."

They met the crowd where the street turned off from the Post Road. It was true—every man and child ashore was coming up the road. In their midst walked Father Amiraux from the French shore and with him a sailor. The sailor satisfied all Greta's ideas of a pirate, even to the gold hoops that dangled from under the scarf knotted around his head.

"Have they captured him or something?" Greta asked excitedly. Retha laughed at her.

"Of course not," she said. "He's probably just a sailor who speaks some other foreign language and they are bringing him to see Anthony. It often happens."

"But you've never told me about Anthony," Greta reminded her. "Did you ask your mother if you might? And why do they bring strange sailors to see him?"

"Mother said it was all right to tell you," Retha said. "I just forgot. It's not a secret, really. But when you came that first day—I didn't know you well enough, I guess. Let's go and tell Mother now that Father Amiraux is here with another sailor."

Mrs. Morrill already knew, and was standing in her doorway. The crowd had surged past the Morrills' to the house where Anthony lived. Father Amiraux and the sailor had gone inside and the men lounged against the fence or sauntered up and down. Women had come out in all the doorways to wait. They talked back and forth but their voices were hushed and there was something solemn about the group waiting in the gray fog.

"I declare," said Mrs. Morrill, "it's like waiting for a death or a new baby. Come inside, girls. We can see from the side window when they come out."

"Greta doesn't know about Anthony," Retha told her mother. "You tell her. You know the story better than I do."

Mrs. Morrill picked up some knitting, but it lay idly in her lap as she talked. "Anthony must be over sixty-five now," she began, "and he's lived here for over forty years—yes, nearer forty-five, I dare say. I was just a creeper when they found him so I only know the story as I've heard it told.

"Old Cap'n Cheney had left some gear on the shore one night and he went down early the next morning to look for it. About daybreak it was. Just around the point he saw a vessel putting out to sea. She'd just put about, and she looked to him like a man o' war—at least that's what he used to say later. Anyhow she was strange enough in these waters to astonish him. But he was more astonished when he heard a moan down by some rocks. He scrambled down to the beach in a hurry and found—Anthony. They say his clothes were elegant and fine and his shirt had ruffles on it. Beside him lay a canteen and some ship's biscuits. He was young, and handsome too, they say, but *his legs had been cut off just above the knees!* The stumps were about healed, but you could tell he'd not been born that way.

"Well, the old Cap'n called for help and they carried him up and put him to bed. He opened his eyes once or twice and made a sound. Some claimed it sounded like he was trying to say 'Anthony' so that's what they called him. He never spoke again," Mrs. Morrill ended, "and that's really all we know about him."

"All?" said Greta. "But, Mrs. Morrill, *why* didn't he speak again? And what had *happened* to him. The story can't end like that."

"Maybe a *story* can't, child," Mrs. Morrill told her. "But *life* can and often does. Oh, we've made all sorts of *guesses* about him. We used to think it was just that he spoke a strange language and couldn't understand ours. And whenever a strange ship put in anywhere along this shore, they'd bring an officer or a sailor up to speak to him. I guess they've tried every lingo under the sun on him, but it's no use. Only Father Amiraux still has hope. Some think that whoever cut off his legs cut the vocal cords in his throat, too, so he never *could* speak—and maybe tell something they didn't want known. But I can't believe that myself. It seems as if he could *write*—if he wanted to, but he never *has*. Still he could have learned to speak our language by this time if he had the power of speech," she added. "It's a puzzle whichever way you look at it."

"But his legs, Mrs. Morrill! You think they were *cut* off? *On purpose?*"

"We don't know that for certain, either, Greta. Some thought they'd been bit off by a shark in tropic seas somewhere. Or maybe there'd been an accident on shipboard. But the doctors who have looked at them all say it was a surgeon's work,. and a skillful surgeon, at that."

"And the man o' war? Hadn't anybody else seen her?"

"That man o' war, or whatever she was, didn't aim to be seen, Greta. She put in for one purpose and then she vanished."

Greta was silent for a minute, thinking.

"What do you believe about him yourself?" she asked.

"I don't know, child. In my day I've believed one thing after another. But no theory holds water. Except," she paused for a minute and then went on slowly, "I can never believe that Anthony is simple. There's a brain and intelligence at work behind those fine eyes. I've always believed he could hear, too, but Retha's father laughs at me. No, Anthony's helpless but he's not hopeless. And he's looking for someone, I'll be bound. Whether it's a friend or a foe, I don't presume to guess. You've noticed how he looks at every stranger? Well, some day I'm hoping that Anthony finds the face he is looking for."

"Mother! You mean someone who's *wronged* him?

So he could take a last revenge?'' Quiet Retha was all excitement.

"Well," her mother answered, "I've never seen a caged eagle, but from descriptions I've heard its eyes must look the way Anthony's have—once or twice in my memory. Revenge—and that sort of thing—is romantic, Retha. What I'd like best would be to see Anthony's face soften just once when those piercing eyes of his fall on someone from home." She smiled at their earnest faces. "I doubt it will ever happen," she concluded.

"It's like a riddle, Mrs. Morrill." Greta was almost in tears. "And every riddle has an answer. There's *got* to be an answer."

"Of course, there's an answer, Greta," Mrs. Morrill told her. "But that doesn't mean *we* need to *know* the answer. Maybe nobody in Blue Cove—or Little Valley, either—will ever know the answer to the mystery of Anthony. And maybe we'll all be just as well off as if we did."

Greta looked at her quickly. The thought of Ann had come to them both at the same moment.

"Did—did the men find—Ann?" she whispered.

Mrs. Morrill didn't speak but she shook her head and there were tears in her eyes.

"Look," she said quickly. "They must be through next door. There's the sailor out on the steps."

They all stepped out to the gate. Father Amiraux stood in the doorway. He raised his hand for attention and everyone edged closer.

"My friends," he said slowly in his tired, pleasant voice. "My friends, the language this sailor speaks is nothing that Anthony can understand."

They made way for him to pass. Someone offered the sailor tobacco, and his teeth flashed in a wide smile. Everyone seemed more relieved than disappointed. They began to talk and laugh a little as they fell in around their visitors to see them aboard their boat.

8. THE VESSEL FROM BOMBAY

SEPTEMBER and October are the golden months of
the year in the province, the fishermen say. There
was hardly a haze on the sea and the Tollerton foghorn
was silent day after day. Greta wondered if she would
get over the mountain again before spring. Even No-
vember was unusually clear.

"Do you think we'll have any more heavy fogs this
season, Father?" she asked him one evening as he sat
milking. She tried to make the question sound casual.

"I doubt it, Greta," he said. "You'd best work hard
at your school work if you are going to write your tenth
year in June," he added. Greta waited for him to say
more. She knew he was just being "fatherly" and not
thinking at all of the tenth year examinations she would
have to take in another year. But he filled the pail to
the brim and gave it to her to carry to the house before
he spoke again. Then, finally, just as she turned away,
he said, "There's disappointment over the mountain,
little girl." His half-smile and the feeling of understanding between them took away the sense of foreboding that lay in the words themselves. Greta smiled
back but she could think of nothing to say.

The winter was a busy one. There was the musicale to practice for, the school play, the benefit entertainment in the Hall; there was Red Cross knitting to be done, and all sorts of war work. Blue Cove and the people there seemed to Greta like something she had read in a book. But spring came early. The ice broke up a month sooner than usual, the men said. And when she opened her eyes one morning to the first dense fog of the season, Greta knew in her heart that the story of Blue Cove might seem like a book she had read, but it was an unfinished book—a book put down unwillingly. The tingling excitement that came with the fog was as strong as ever within her.

A month went by before a Saturday afternoon and a fog came conveniently together.

"I'd hoped you'd outgrown that nonsense of going off alone in the fog," her mother said, but she offered no real objection.

Greta wondered a little, as she sped along the familiar lane toward the fork, if an adventure like hers could have outlived the winter. Or had it been something so fragile that it would winterkill like other lovely, delicate things? It was an effort to look toward the spot where Old Man Himion's house would stand if all were well. But it was there—its sharp pointed gable rising unmistakably among the spruces. Blue Cove, too, would be waiting for her.

The Old Road was more washed out than ever after the spring rains. There were low places or spots crossed by streams where you had to jump from rock to rock. Road building in the early days must have been a gigantic task if it required such stones as these for a foundation. But once across the high pasture it was smoother going. Tollerton was silent here and the road was in good repair. The road commissioner might have finished only yesterday.

The village street looked the same as usual and Princess sat watching at the Morrills' gate. With her heart thumping Greta burst into the kitchen and flung herself into Mrs. Morrill's arms. It was as if she had just come home from a voyage, and there were long, long days of separation to be crushed out of existence. Mrs. Morrill was glad to see her but she seemed surprised, and Greta reminded herself that time meant nothing in Blue Cove.

"Why, Greta, you've been running," Mrs. Morrill laughed. "Did you see a bear in the clearing? Ronnie and Edgar saw one a week ago near the Sentinel Rocks, and Guy saw one yesterday when he brought the mail down. But they never do you any harm."

"I'm just glad to be here, that's all," Greta told her. Mrs. Morrill smoothed back her hair with the quick stroke that Greta liked.

"I see," was all she said but she looked at Greta

closely. "You are growing up," she added as if she had only just noticed it. "When will you be twelve?"

Greta was troubled. "In the fall," she answered. "But why did you ask me—just that way, Mrs. Morrill? I mean—you didn't ask me how old I was—but when I'd be twelve."

Mrs. Morrill dropped down into the Loyalist rocker and drew Greta to her. She did not try to explain what lay back in her own childhood that made her so sure Greta was under twelve.

"Don't you *want* to be twelve?" she asked.

"I don't know," Greta said honestly. "I always think of my birthdays as a flight of stairs," she went on a little shyly. "Up to twelve it's been fun to look up. But after twelve—the stairs turn. I can't see around the bend."

"I know," Mrs. Morrill said. "Not *now*, you can't. But when you get to that twelfth step you *will* be able to see 'around the bend,' as you put it. Seeing ahead, or looking ahead—is something we do with our hearts— it takes nothing but time and courage. The one is given to us; the other we must provide." It was never so much what Mrs. Morrill said as the quiet, understanding way in which she spoke that Greta found comforting. And now she let all vague dread of the dignity and importance of being twelve slip from her.

"That's right," Mrs. Morrill smiled approvingly as she watched Greta's face brighten. "And now I have something to tell you. Princess has had some kittens since you were here," she said. "I'd like you to have one when they are older. They haven't got their eyes open yet but you can see them next time you come."

"Oh, I'd *love* a kitten—specially one of Princess's!" Greta was delighted until a thought came to her. "Could I—could I keep it—do you think?" she asked. The same thought must have crossed Mrs. Morrill's mind, too, because she said "Oh" and then hesitated. "Well, we'll think about it," she added. "But you had better run along now to find Retha. She's down at the shore. Something must have happened down there, I guess. I heard Burton and Kelsey calling her to come a while back."

Down on the beach it was very quiet. Greta passed two ox teams left standing in the middle of the road; the smith had left his forge and the store was empty. She ran out onto the wharf. Here they all were, gathered in groups or pacing slowly up and down—an unusually silent throng of men and children looking out to sea. She found Retha among them.

"Retha," she whispered, "what's happened? Has there been an accident?"

"No," Retha told her. "But, can you see? There's a big vessel standing off shore. And we don't know what she is."

Greta could just make out a vague pattern of masts

and spars where Retha was pointing. "Yes, I can see," she said. "But why is everyone so—so kind of—solemn?"

"I don't know," Retha whispered back. "It's funny, isn't it? But the men seem to think there's something strange about her. They've sent a dory out to see what she is. Old Mr. Morehouse has gone, and two others. They say she's too big to land at this wharf even if it were clear enough to get in."

They settled down to wait for the dory. The men talked in low voices. The vessel off shore might have been a ghost ship for the spell it cast. No one seemed to know why, but they waited on the wharf as shrouded in foreboding as they were in fog. When a gull mewed overhead they stirred nervously, and when their ears caught the creaking of oars, everyone surged to the edge to look over. The elder men gathered at the top of the iron ladder. Mr. Morehouse came up first and the rest of the dory's crew followed him onto the wharf. They stood in a close group and spoke together. One or two others were summoned, and the talking continued. Something at last seemed decided, and old Mr. Morehouse stepped out from among them as spokesman. He took off his cap before he began to speak and stood bareheaded before them.

"She's the *Emmeretta,* folks, Cap'n Cornwall's vessel," he told them.

The *Emmeretta!* Why the *Emmeretta* was almost one of their own, sailing as she did out of Middle Harbour, not five miles up the shore. No mystery about *her* —except having Captain Ansel Cornwall anchor off shore here instead of going on home. They murmured among themselves and then were silent as Mr. Morehouse began to speak again.

"Mrs. Cornwall's in command of her," he went on.

"*Mrs.* Cornwall! Laleah Cornwall!" They couldn't believe it. She was no seafaring woman. This was her first voyage. She had gone as a bride from this very town on her honeymoon to the Far East. Even the children could remember the gay wedding not two years before. Captain Cornwall had at last won the bride that he had courted between voyages for twenty years.

To Greta the names "Cornwall" and "Laleah Cornwall" seemed familiar. Where had she heard them? There was no one of that name living in Little Valley. But she stopped wondering to listen to the people around her.

"But the Cap'n? Where's he?" voices asked.

"Cap'n Cornwall died aboard ship. He died in the roadstead of Bombay," Mr. Morehouse continued slowly.

"But why's Laleah Cornwall bringing the vessel home? Where's the mate?" someone asked quickly.

"Young Eldridge, the mate, is my wife's cousin," another added.

"There's been trouble aboard." There was complete silence as the old man went on. "Cap'n Cornwall died in his own cabin. But he died of—of *yellow fever*. The mate wanted to bury him at sea as was right and proper. And then, I reckon, Laleah Cornwall went mad. You can understand how it'd be. She'd been married but a few months. Well, she got hold of the Cap'n's pistols and she threatened to kill every man in the crew if they didn't do her bidding. She swore she'd bring the Cap'n home for Christian burial in her family plot. There was no sense to it, of course, but she held the only firearms aboard. She meant what she said. And they knew it.

"Young Eldridge was between the devil and the deep sea—a crazed woman holding two guns on him and a crew well-nigh out of its wits with terror as long as the Cap'n's body was aboard. But he played a man's part, I'll say that for him, and he thought fast. He thought up a plan and he persuaded Laleah Cornwall to agree to it. Between them he and the ship's carpenter got the Cap'n sewed up in sailcloth; they lashed the body in the ship's longboat and they towed the Cap'n home. Young Eldridge says that Mrs. Cornwall never put her guns down until they were cleared for the open sea; and she kept vigil over that line for days for fear somebody'd cut the longboat loose. I guess after a time she must have let down a bit. She could see the crew was content—as long as there was a line between them and the longboat. It would have been a different story, though, if anybody else had been struck down with the fever. That would have started the panic all over again. She's quiet enough now," he added. "She's a broken-hearted woman, and sort of dazed from all she's been through. But she's clear enough in her mind. And she wants to bury the Cap'n in her family's plot rather than where his folks lie. Rupert, Burpee, and the rest of us here have agreed to let her. There's no danger now after the months the longboat's been tossing in the tropic sun. But we'll send someone down the shore to ask Dr. Ingraham for certain so the womenfolk won't fret about the children."

There was no unwillingness, only murmurs of sympathy. The men broke up into groups to discuss it and make plans.

"Like as not Laleah Cornwall will feel more comfortable in her own home," one said. "I'll go tell the womenfolk. My wife and some of the others can get her house open and aired out before Laleah comes ashore."

"My wife'll be glad to help," said another. "A house that's been closed for over a year is a gloomy place to come back to."

Mr. Morehouse gave directions. Young men were dispatched to row up the shore to Middle Harbour to carry the news of the *Emmeretta's* homecoming. Others were sent down shore to tell the minister; and to ask if Doctor Ingraham thought it safe to bury a victim of yellow fever ashore.

Only Greta could be quite sure of the answer they would bring back. Suddenly it had come to her why the names of the captain and his wife were so familiar. Over the mountain, in her own village cemetery, among the oldest headstones, were two that bore the names *Captain Ansel Cornwall* and *Laleah Cornwall, Widow of Captain Ansel Cornwall*.

Retha and Greta trouped slowly back along the beach with the others. No one had heart to go back to work. Only from one small building on the shore came familiar sounds. The carpenter was already hard at work sawing up his best lumber. He was building a coffin for Captain Ansel Cornwall. When you build a vessel to go out to meet the sea, you put into it only the finest timber and the finest workmanship; the vessel must match the integrity of the men who sail it. Surely this last little barque, destined to withstand not the sea but the soil, must be fashioned with the same integrity. The helpless body sewn in sailcloth and lying out there in the longboat in the fog had come half around the world to rest in its native soil. It must have the finest coffin the carpenter could build.

As they listened to the pounding, the older men were

all thinking of the gay Cornwall wedding and that honeymoon to foreign lands. Laleah Cornwall had been proud and headstrong. Yes, and vain, too, the women always said. Only a vain woman would relish sending her lover off to sea again and again as she had done for the pleasure of seeing him come back faithfully at the end of each voyage. They wondered if it was regret for all the lost years that had driven the bride to such frenzied courage that she had dared to defy the crew and bring the Captain home. Well, she was a young woman still. There would be many years to regret the folly of her youth.

But Greta knew better. Only she, in all Blue Cove, knew that on the tombstone in the cemetery the dates showed that Laleah Cornwall had survived her husband by less than a year.

The next day in Little Valley was as foggy as the one before had been. Tollerton foghorn had not stopped its steady warning blasts once during the night. It was Sunday, too, and it should be the day of Captain Cornwall's funeral.

All during the morning Greta could not keep her mind from the drama going on over the mountain. She wanted, yet hesitated to go. Perhaps when she got there it would not be the "next" day in Blue Cove at all; perhaps there would be no reference whatever to the *Emmeretta's* homecoming. But she had to find out.

"I don't like your going for walks on a Sunday," her mother said.

"Just this once, Mother," Greta begged. "And I promise I'll be back in plenty of time for Young People's meeting."

At the fork Old Man Himion's house showed plainly. But there was no smoke from his chimney and ahead of her, where the Old Road entered the spruce woods, she thought she saw his tall figure merge with the fog. Old Man Himion, too, was going to the Captain's funeral.

As she passed the Sentinel Rocks, Greta could see people coming up from the shore. They had come from up and down the coast in their boats and they were climbing the steep road from the wharf in solemn, hushed little groups. Unwilling to meet so many strangers, she walked slowly until they had all turned into the street. By the time she reached the clearing they were out of sight in the fog.

She found Retha in the doorway with Princess in her arms. There were children in the other doorways, too, and they called to Greta in hushed voices. Anthony had crawled to his favorite spot inside the fence and he kept the babies he was minding very quiet.

"Mother said I could stay outside until the procession leaves the church," Retha told her. "Then I'm to go inside so as not to seem curious about others' sorrow."

It was so quiet that they could hear the murmur of voices from the church at the end of the street. Princess had slipped down to curl gracefully on the stone doorstep.

"So many of the things that happen here seem *sad* things," Greta said finally.

Retha looked at her in astonishment. "Isn't there sorrow where *you* live?" she asked.

"Of course," Greta was forced to admit.

"But less than here?" Retha wanted to know.

"I don't know. No—I guess not."

Retha seemed relieved. "My mother says that living and dying are such natural things that one shouldn't be any more sorrowful than the other. Unless they are deaths because of a war. That's different, of course. I mean, when—when people die that way it isn't natural—or it isn't part of what she calls everyday living. But, thank goodness, we don't have to be afraid of war. There's no need for our country ever, ever to have another war, is there?"

Greta thought of the war that was shadowing the whole world and she groped helplessly for a reply.

"But sometimes somebody else makes you fight when you don't want to. You just *have* to fight," she tried to explain.

"That's silly," said Retha. "Nobody has to fight." Greta knew she could never explain to Retha the riddle of her generation. She was relieved to see that the service was over. Through the fog came a slow procession.

They slipped indoors and the other children did the same. Only Anthony stayed outside, peering through the pickets of the fence with his strange questioning eyes.

It was a small procession that followed the coffin along the village street to the old Post Road and turned east to go over the mountain. Laleah Cornwall walked straight and proud in her widow's weeds; friends and relatives followed, and the *Emmeretta's* crew, awkward in their shore clothes, came at the end. When she was sure that she would be in no danger of overtaking it, Greta started home over the mountain.

Late that afternoon, when the Young People's meeting in her own church parlor was over, Greta slipped out into the cemetery and stepped quietly between the familiar graves. But there was no fresh mound there, unsodded and recent.

9. THE GOVERNMENT HOUSE BALL

GRETA often wished that she could hear more about the persons she met or saw or became interested in at Blue Cove. Sometimes things happened while she was there that were as exciting as a cinema and she felt as she did once or twice when she had had to leave before a picture was finished. Sometimes it was like stepping into a cinema near the end of a picture when she could only guess at all that had gone before. The Morrills were willing enough to answer questions, but often Greta had a queer feeling that even they might not know the answers. Perhaps she herself sometimes knew better than they. Surely this was true about Ann and it was true, too, about the widow of Captain Cornwall. Laleah Cornwall was a favorite topic of conversation among the women who brought their knitting or mending over to Mrs. Morrill's pleasant kitchen on foggy afternoons. At such times Greta would sit on the floor with Princess in her lap and listen as they discussed the widow Cornwall. Laleah was a rich woman now. She could even have as smart a pair of horses as Mrs. Trask's if she wished. Would she marry again? they wondered, or would she be content to stay on in her girlhood home

and grow old, another of the solitary widows with
whom the province abounds? The tongues of her neighbors might have been softer if they had known that,
worn out by genuine grief, she was so soon to follow the
captain over the mountain to the cemetery on the other
side. But only Greta knew that.

There were some questions that Greta was sure her
father could answer. What, for instance, had happened
to the village of Blue Cove itself? Prosperous villages
didn't turn into a cluster of sod-covered cellar holes
over night. If some persons in such towns made fortunes
and moved away, there were always others to stay on
and live and die in the homes of their fathers. But it
was a question she could never ask.

Perhaps the strangest part of all this queer and lovely
experience was that she was sure in her heart that her
father as a boy had known Blue Cove as she knew it.
She had caught a look on his face sometimes when she
had come home in the early dusk of a foggy day that was
more than welcome. It was more like the way her mother
had looked when Greta had come home once from a
visit to grandmother's—an eager look, begging for news
of loved ones. Once, too, Father had brought some gentians from a trip inland.

" 'Her eyes are as blue as the gentian,' " he quoted,
and then added, "did you ever see eyes as blue as the gentian, Greta?"

"Never except Mrs. Morriil's," Greta had answered without thinking and caught her breath for fear he would ask some embarrassing question. But he didn't. Still, why had she been so sure that he heard and understood and was pleased? His only reply had been to tell her, quite casually, that the gentians would look well in the pink luster pitcher.

But Greta seldom wasted time in wondering. She was busy and happy in clear weather. And if the strange fog —born as it was of the northern ice and the tropic sea —had a magic power to enfold her in another life, she saw no need to be anything but happy there, too.

It was very pleasant to find Retha waiting for her at the Sentinel Rocks one day and looking unusually excited for such a quiet girl. "I just couldn't have borne it if you hadn't come today!" were her first words. "What do you think's happened?" she went on. She gave Greta no chance to speak. "Mrs. Stanton is back from Halifax! She's at Mrs. Trask's and she's coming over to tea!"

Greta was just as excited. "Did she see the Duke of Kent?" she asked.

"We don't *know*, but she must have, because she looks so happy. Anyhow she laughed when Mother asked her. And now you'll be here when she tells us about it! I've got to hurry right back. I promised Mother I'd butter the bread for tea. She will slice it because I never can get it thin enough, and you can help me butter it. We'll need *loads* of it because everybody's coming."

They raced on down the Old Road together and turned into the village street. Anthony was peering out between the pickets in his fence corner with such a piercing look that Retha stopped suddenly. She always treated him as if he could hear and understand.

"Mrs. Stanton has come back from Halifax, Anthony," she said distinctly and in that louder tone we always use to foreigners. "We don't know for sure, but we *think* she got what she went after. Anyhow I'll tell you tomorrow." A little flicker of a smile lightened Anthony's somber face. Greta could not tell whether it meant that he had understood or whether it was merely his response to a friendly gesture.

Indoors Mrs. Morrill had opened the parlor and was putting little touches to her spotless house. The butter had been brought up from the cellar to soften, and preserves and dishes of candied ginger were set out. The delicate task of buttering the thin slices of soft bread kept both girls busy until after the guests had begun to arrive.

All the neighbors were there who had been there on that Sunday afternoon when Mrs. Stanton had stopped on her way to Halifax. There were others besides so that the parlor was filled and some even sat in the kitchen.

Mrs. Trask, impatient as always with any preliminary conversation, said briskly, "Well, Ardis, did you see the Duke?"

Mrs. Stanton nodded happily. "Yes," she said, "I saw him," and paused.

"Well, go *on*, Ardis Stanton!" Mrs. Trask bade. "We aim to hear more than that you stood and gaped at him. Even a cat can look at a queen."

Mrs. Stanton only laughed. "I must tell my story in my own way, Harriet Trask," she said. "You always did hurry me. In school you stood better than I did and I always thought it was because you never gave me a chance to answer." The others laughed, too.

"Take your own time, Ardis," Stella Denton said. "Like as not we'll survive the suspense even if it doesn't seem possible now."

"I reached Halifax pretty well worn out," Mrs. Stanton began slowly. "But you wouldn't be so much interested in what happened to me on the way. I walked most of it. Oh, I had a few rides but it seemed best to save what money I had for food and decent lodgings. At Annapolis Royal and at Windsor I had friends to stop with, so I could rest up and start out fresh again.

"I told you when I was here that I had a plan for seeing the Duke. I hardly dared hope it would work. But it did. Old Mr. Blackthorn, down on the Island, has a grandniece in service in Government House and he gave me a note to her. She turned out to be a pleasant girl and she promised to help me. Now this was my plan —*somehow* I had to get into Government House when there was a party; and *somehow* I had to be presented to His Highness. I knew there was no use in applying for an audience on business. I'd never have got past all the guards and aides and secretaries with my clothes and my story—no, nor with my wrinkles, either. But I had one dress—my wedding dress. My grandfather brought that ivory silk all the way from China for my sixteenth birthday. He said then it was to be laid aside for my wedding dress. I remember Mother thought it wasn't suitable and that it was too elegant, but when I came to get married two years later, Grandfather made quite a fuss. She finally let me use it."

"That was as lovely a length of silk as ever came out of the East, Ardis," Mrs. Denton interrupted. "Captain Dakin must have enjoyed picking it out. But then he always favored you."

"I guess he must have," Mrs. Stanton agreed. "I used to tell Mother she was just a mite envious of that silk. Of course, I knew she *wasn't*, but you know how proper she always was and how everything had to be what she called 'suitable.' And that ivory brocade, *she* said, was only 'suitable' for a court ball. Well, one day last winter when it seemed that I'd about reached the end of my strength, I went into my room and took my wedding dress out of the chest. It was the only pretty thing I had left and it used to rest me to sit and hold it. It took me back—but you know how that is. A dress you've worn and been happy in always gathers in and holds a sort of fragrance of happiness. I got to thinking how Grandfather and Mother had argued about using that silk for my wedding. All at once it came to me what Mother had said about its being suitable for a court ball. I made up my mind I'd see the Duke of Kent in that dress."

The women all laughed. Young Prince Edward, Duke of Kent and the King's own son, who had just come out to the province, had shown a marked preference for ladies who were beautiful. Even as far from Halifax as the islands off the Neck, stories of his taste for beauty had spread.

"Well, I call *that* using the wits the Lord gave you," Mrs. Trask laughed. "Go on, Ardis. How did you contrive to do it?"

"I knew I'd have to dress inside of Government House," Mrs. Stanton continued. "If I was to arrive on foot and unescorted, the guards would be sure to question me. Besides, I had no proper wrap to wear and I couldn't flounce through the streets of Halifax in my brocade. And there's where Cynthia Blackthorn helped. She had got a cousin of hers to give me lodging. One night when she went back to Government House after

her time off, she took my package along. She smuggled it
in and hid it in one of the linen presses.

"I had to wait nearly a week before my chance came.
It would never do to risk my plan on a small affair.
But I watched the bulletin of news from Government
House and Cynthia listened to all the inside chatter until a truly big ball was announced. Why, there were to
be guests from as far away as Shelbourne and Digby!
When the night came Cynthia smuggled me in, tucked
me into a clothes press and brought me my gown. Poor
young one! She was excited as a child at the idea of my
masquerading as a guest, but scared, too. Such a prank
might well have lost her her place. Well, I smoothed my
hair, changed in the dark, and waited. When Cynthia
came for me she was laughing. She was holding a perfect
yellow rose. It must have dropped from some lady's
bouquet, and I took it as a sign that my plan was going
to succeed. I *knew* it. I slipped the rose into the coil of
my hair and it was all I needed with Grandmother's earrings. Cynthia said His Highness was expected at any
moment. He was driving down from his estate up at
Bedford on the Basin, and an outrider had just ridden
in with word that the coach had started.

"The guests were lining up in the hall. Cynthia took
me down a little stair that came out near the foot of the
grand staircase. I elbowed my way, as politely as I could,

into the front line. I wasn't one to risk failure by hanging back now, so I kept my eyes fixed on the entrance and pretended I didn't hear the indignant little snorts and questions of the ladies around me.

"Oh, I wish you could all have seen that hall. Lights, music, mirrors, flowers and silks! It was all I could do to keep my head. His Highness arrived just in time to keep me from swooning, I guess, from something like intoxication. He is a handsome young man, tall and slender as a prince should be; and, bowing and smiling, he was a fine sight. The line swept into a deep curtsy with a swish of silk that almost drowned out the violins. When he came to me, I edged out a few inches and I saw to it that I caught his eye. He gave me a sharp glance and I could tell he had marked me. When he passed by and the lines broke up and surged up the staircase to the ball room, I declare I think my heart stopped beating. I tried to act as if I belonged there and as if my escort had only just left me for a moment. I don't know how long it was before I felt a touch on my arm. His Highness had sent an aide for me! He wished to be presented!"

The women had dropped their knitting. They were listening spellbound, seeing in their minds the vivid, colorful picture of a grand ball.

"I had caught his eye. Now I knew I must catch his *ear*," Mrs. Stanton went on. "I gave him no chance to discover for himself that I was an impostor. I told him at once that I came uninvited, but that I had walked two hundred miles to see him and to get justice; that I trusted him to help me. He was surprised—flattered, perhaps. He hesitated just a moment and frowned a little; then he smiled, bowed graciously and directed his aide to take me to a reception room to await his leisure to hear my story.

"I must have waited two hours in what seemed like another world. There was a French window in the room and it opened on the gardens. I could hear the music from the ball room. Once a servant came with refreshments. His Highness had not forgotten me. When he came at last, he was in good humor, gay and interested. There was an officer with him and a secretary to take notes. He heard me through, asked a few questions, assured me that he believed me, that he would investigate and see that justice was done. 'Where was I staying?' I gave my address. 'Would it be convenient for me to remain in Halifax for a short time until he could confer with Governor Wentworth and have the necessary papers prepared?' I assured him it would. 'Good. He would attend to it at once. And now would I care to mingle with the guests or prefer to have his aide escort me home?' 'I should prefer to leave at once,' I told him, and the interview was over."

Every woman in Laura Morrill's parlor gave a little sigh of satisfaction.

"And the papers actually came?" they asked.

"Yes, less than a week later," Mrs. Stanton told them. "An aide brought them, with a bouquet, a purse 'to defray the expenses of my journey,' and a note from His Highness to the effect that 'he hoped to take a cruise around the province in the *Zebra* the following spring and would at that time assure himself that I was happily in possession of my property.' But here they are—the note and the papers. Read them yourselves! I pressed a few of the flowers, too, to persuade myself and the children that it all happened."

"Well, the young man certainly does nothing by halves," said Harriet Trask.

"Ardis Stanton," old Mrs. Morehouse's cool voice broke in on the chatter and questions that filled the room as the women examined the note and the papers with their crests and seals. "Ardis Stanton, I've told you that you were the loveliest bride I ever saw in my lifetime. I'd like to see you again as you looked on your wedding day in your ivory brocade. Will you put it on, my dear?"

Mrs. Stanton looked startled. But the others urged.

"Why, I'd just as leave," she said. "It won't take but a minute. No, don't you bother to come with me, Harriet," to Mrs. Trask. "I can manage alone. I had to at Government House, you know."

As soon as she was safely out of hearing, Mrs. Denton

said, "Isn't there something we can do to celebrate? It seems as if this is an occasion to remember after all Ardis's hard times."

"We can have candlelight, can't we, Laura?" Mrs. Morehouse asked Mrs. Morrill. "There was candlelight for her wedding. And her ivory gown and ivory skin will look their best by candlelight."

"Of course we can, Mrs. Morehouse. Will you all help? The extra candlesticks stand in the bottom of the corner cupboard. Just put them around everywhere. And, Retha, run over to the Saunders. If Grandfather Saunders is home, ask him to come quick with his fiddle. Greta, you come with me and we'll pick honeysuckle. Get out all the ginger jars and bowls you can find, Stella," she called back to Mrs. Denton, "and fill them with water."

The honeysuckle vine that covered the east side of the house was in full bloom. Mrs. Morrill stood on a cask and cut long sprays of the red and yellow blossoms with a lavish hand. She sent Greta hurrying indoors with armfuls. "These are for the ginger jars," she told her. "Tell Stella Denton to arrange them."

When Greta returned, she found Mrs. Morrill shaping more of the blossoms into a stiff, old-fashioned bouquet. "This will have to serve as the bride's bouquet," she said. "I'm sorry it hasn't a lace frill; but it will blend well with the ivory brocade at any rate. Run back, Greta, so you can see Ardis when she comes. I'll take this to her."

Greta slipped back into the house. All in a moment it had been transformed. A dozen twinkling candles had worked their magic. Clusters of the red and yellow honeysuckle, as foreign as the ginger jars that held it, trailed from familiar shelves and cupboards and filled the room with heavy perfume. A door closed near by. "S—s—sh," someone said, and they all stood quietly.

There was a sound of footsteps and then Ardis Stanton appeared. From somewhere out in back, Grandfather Saunders was playing softly on his fiddle. Framed in the doorway, Mrs. Stanton stood facing her old neighbors and girlhood friends. She hardly knew whether to laugh or cry, and the little half-smile on her face was becoming; it softened and gentled the lines that bitterness had carved. Curious gold earrings that reached almost to her shoulders hung from under the smooth sweep of black hair; and her roughened hands were hidden by lace mitts and by the round bouquet of honeysuckle. But the ivory brocade! It seemed to glow with a light all its own—to give off a soft radiance like some of the strange creatures of the sea. Greta could see how it must have bewitched the old sea captain bargaining for it in some dim Canton warehouse. No wonder it had arrested, if not bewitched, the young Duke of Kent.

Mrs. Trask put into words what she and the others were thinking.

"I declare, Ardis, you *are* a beauty still. And I'm not surprised you came back with the papers. The Duke would have had to be blind in both eyes not to relish the picture you make in that gown."

But Mrs. Stanton was very near tears. Her mind had gone back beyond her recent triumph. She was thinking of the day of her wedding when she had stepped out in her bridal gown with fine Aubry Stanton at her side and all life ahead of them.

Old Mrs. Morehouse had the gift of seeing with her heart as well as her eyes. Her mind, too, had traveled swiftly back, past the scene in Halifax to the girlhood of Ardis Stanton.

"Ardis," she said, "Aubry Stanton would be as proud of you today as he was fifteen years ago when he saw you first in that gown. Yes, and more so, my dear. The courage of a fine woman is more in the sight of God and men than the beauty of a lovely girl, and Aubry Stanton would be one to know it."

Mrs. Stanton sent her a grateful look that said more than any words she could force to her lips. She smiled through her tears. The moment of reminiscence was folded away—not to be forgotten but to be stored with the other treasured moments that the ivory brocade held in its luminous folds. A pleasant little buzz of conversation broke out. Grandfather Saunders swung into a gayer tune and there was soft laughter and the gentle clatter of tea things.

Greta looked slowly from one face to another in the room. Never before had she seen so many of the folk of Blue Cove together—never before had she felt so close to them, so much a part of their life, as she did today in this candlelit room. When her eyes reached Mrs. Morrill, she found that she was beckoning to her. Greta slipped over to her side, and Mrs. Morrill drew her close to her for a moment.

"I'm glad you have been here today," she said. "But —the wind has changed, Greta. It will blow off the fog in another half hour. You had best be on your way over the mountain. I am sorry you can't stay to have tea with us. But I'll give you some bread and butter with a bit of wild strawberry preserves to eat as you go."

She went to the door with her. Greta stood outside looking down at the marking on the curious stone slab that lay in front of the door. She never could find words, somehow, to say good-by to Mrs. Morrill; perhaps, because the only words that wanted to come to her lips were always, "Shall I see you again?" Mrs. Morrill tilted Greta's chin up in a quick gesture. Greta looked into the clear blue eyes so like the eyes of the old sea captains who looked on far horizons.

"You know I wouldn't send you away if I could help it, Greta," Mrs. Morrill said quietly. And then she added, "I wouldn't send you away—*ever*. Go now, my dear, *quickly*."

Greta turned at the end of the street to wave. The changing wind was blowing the fog in thick swirls along the street. She could see that Mrs. Morrill was still standing at the door, but her figure was blurred and indistinct—already merging into mystery. Greta did not look back again. She wanted to keep in her heart the picture of that gay room filled with happy, kindly women in their rustling best silks. But most of all she wanted to keep the picture of Laura Morrill standing in her doorway and seeing her off. She felt that she could never bear to lose that. She hurried out into the Old Road and followed it upward over the mountain.

10. GRETA'S TWELFTH BIRTHDAY

G RETA's twelfth birthday was very near and she
thought about it often. She couldn't explain even
to herself why it seemed so important. She wondered if
the other girls felt about a twelfth birthday as she did,
and one day she worked up her courage to ask Christine
Frosst who lived next door. Christine was an older girl,
serious and earnest. Greta caught her alone one morning at the well.

"Christine, tell me something," she began. "Do you
remember how you felt on your twelfth birthday? Was
it any different from other birthdays?"

Christine set her full pail down carefully on the plat-
form and replaced the board with the rock on it over
the top of the well before she answered.

"Yes," she said slowly, "I can remember. My twelfth
birthday seemed terribly important to me."

"Why?" Greta asked eagerly. "And *was* it different
from the others when it came? Going into your 'teens,
I mean?"

"It was the nicest birthday I ever had," Christine
told her, "and yours will be, too. You'll see. Maybe it's
just because you feel that you've accomplished some-

thing, like beating around the Cape in a stiff gale. Or like turning the heel of a sock," she finished. They both laughed as Christine's thoughts crashed so prosaically to earth. "Anyhow," she defended herself, "I *have* turned the heel of a sock so I *know* about that, even if I haven't rounded the Cape."

Greta felt better about the approaching day. She had even begun to look forward to it a little when her father brought home the word that the Committee had decided to hold the annual church picnic at Blue Cove on that day.

"But that's my birthday," she protested.

Both Walter and Gertrude laughed at her. "You didn't expect the world would stop running to celebrate, did you?" Father teased. "However important it is to us three," he added seriously enough to soothe her feelings. "Of course, I could ask the Trustees to reconsider the date if you like," he went on. "But it would be too bad. The tide's just right so that all the fishing boats will be in early. The following week wouldn't be nearly so good for them. But it's for you to say. It's your birthday."

"Father, don't be *silly*. You know you couldn't change the picnic. Of course it doesn't really matter, only it's a shame to have two good times come at once. That's all I meant. You know it is."

Father only grinned at her, but her mother said, "I'd

planned to have you ask Hazen and Frieda, and Marguerite and Gladys and Lyman, and whoever else you want, for tea on your birthday. You can have them just as well a day or two later and that will spread the good times along."

"Oh, thank you, Mother. I'll love having a party sometime in the next week. Saturday can be my private birthday—my secret one—and the day of the party will be my public one."

The church picnics were not held in the clearing at Blue Cove, but over on a high point to the left of the beach. It was the favorite spot of the minister of the Little Valley church. His parishioners chose it out of their fondness for him. To reach it you turned off the Old Road below the village clearing, crossed a burned patch, and followed a little footpath up across a windswept headland fragrant with bayberry. It led you out at last to a great open rolling space high above the sea. The ground covering of cranberries and a half dozen interwoven mosses was as springy as a mattress. It reminded the Reverend Mr. Clute of the downs of southern England, looking out across the Channel. But he liked to bring his people here for another reason. He knew that it offered everything the spirit needed for nourishment. On a clear day—with the sea a deep blue, with a crisp wind fanning the excitement of living, with gulls whirling in vast circles and mewing faintly from their great height—on such moments in this place the idea of freedom became so real that you could almost grasp it in your two hands.

Greta decided as the afternoon sped on that it was a perfect way to spend one's twelfth birthday. There was only one thing lacking. If she could somehow have had both her own people and her friends of the Blue Cove village, her happiness would be complete. But there seemed no chance of it. The day remained as clear as crystal. The games, the supper, the singing of familiar songs followed one after another.

They were still singing when a change came in the air. Mothers reached for sweaters to slip on the smaller children and the men began to gather up the picnic baskets that must be carried back to the old Post Road. The little procession was soon on its way up across the headland, anxious, now that it had started, to reach the road before dusk fell. Walter Addington was the last to leave and Greta waited for him. They followed the little path silently, listening to the laughter, the snatches of song, the fretful cries of tired children ahead. Where the path dipped down away from the sea, Greta and her father stopped to look back. They watched the sun slip quietly out of sight, leaving a pattern of opal tints.

"Look yonder—off toward Big Gulch, Greta. Do you see?" her father asked.

Around the point came the first billow of incoming

fog. Almost at the same moment Tollerton's hoarse blasts began down in the Passage.

"It's going to be a foggy night after all, isn't it?" Greta tried to keep out of her voice the little tingle of excitement she felt, but her father must have caught it.

"Happy?" he asked in a very casual tone of voice. "Will it do—for a twelfth birthday?"

"It's been a perfect day, Father, every bit of it," Greta told him, and she gave his arm a happy squeeze as they followed the others.

By the time they reached the Old Road and the baskets and small children were loaded into the ox carts that stood waiting for them, little tendrils of fog were noticeable on the beach. They stole around the big rocks; they blew in soft wisps up the roadway; as sure as the tide, the fog was coming to enfold them, but it was a wayward thing that must play with them first.

The climbing was steep for the first part of the walk back and only a few of the lustier people had breath for song. The others plodded along steadily to the rhythmic sound of the distant foghorn. It was quiet enough to hear the murmur of the stream by the roadside and the sleepy chirping of the birds. As they passed the entrance to the clearing Greta looked in. It was empty. Not yet had the fog reached it to touch it with life. Greta had a sudden impulse. Like throwing out an anchor she dropped her sweater by the side of the road and went on.

Everyone stopped for breath at the top of the mountain and looked back along the road they had come. Gone by now was the horizon, the sea and the shore. Fifty feet behind hung a thick gray curtain through which nothing showed but the dim outlines of spruce trees and the Sentinel Rocks. The ox carts began to creak again and the people got under way. They were singing again on the down hill stretch toward their warm, comfortable homes in Little Valley.

"Father, I must go back for a minute. I—left my sweater," Greta said. Her father gave her a long look.

"Must you?" he asked. Greta didn't answer. Would he offer to go back with her? Would he tell her to leave her sweater? That she could come back in the daytime for it? After a long pause, he said in a matter-of-fact voice, "Run back and get it, Greta. But remember it's late. Don't stay long tonight. I'll wait for you below at the Ezra Knoll."

Greta watched him out of sight. She stood perfectly still where she was until the fog reached her. Then she turned and ran back over the road she had come. She had never been over here quite so late before, but the lateness only made it more exciting. At the entrance into the clearing, she stopped. It was there! The fog that could blot out and take away scenes and landmarks could also give them back. It had given her back the village of Blue Cove!

A light in every house, blurred and uncertain, but warm and friendly, marked the curve of the familiar little street. Homely sounds, a dog barking, the distant closing of a door came to her muffled in the fog. But there was no sound of the foghorn; that had ceased. She ran along the gravel path to Mrs. Morrill's door, and stepped into the kitchen. Mrs. Morrill turned in surprise.

"Why, Greta! How late, child, for you to be here! But I'm glad to see you—always," she added.

"We've been having our church picnic over south of the beach," Greta explained. "And then the fog came in —and the others have gone on. But I—I had to come back. And oh, Mrs. Morrill, it's my twelfth birthday today!"

"Your twelfth birthday, my dear!" Mrs. Morrill looked aghast for a moment, but she added quickly, "Well, I might have known it would come sooner or later. Has it been a happy day?" she asked.

'Oh, yes," Greta told her, "and especially now that I could come here for a minute, even if I can't stay. I wanted to see you today—terribly."

Mrs. Morrill gave her the slow, steady smile that was

as reassuring, as trustworthy as the ray of light from a lighthouse.

"Retha will be sorry she missed you. She's gone up the shore a way with her father. They'll be home soon but you mustn't wait. And, Greta, child, I am glad, too, to have you come in on your twelfth birthday. I have a present for you. But I want especially to wish you 'safe passage.' "

" 'Safe passage?' But—but that's what you say when —when people go off on a voyage!"

"You *are* starting on a voyage, Greta! The happiest voyage in the world—the voyage into your 'teens. But I mustn't let you stay tonight. Wait here, child, while I get the present I have for you."

Greta stood in the middle of the kitchen drinking in its warmth, its friendliness. Her eyes rested on one familiar thing after another; the corner cupboard with the two egg cups side by side in the center of the lower shelf like a baby's first teeth; Grandfather Tidd's glowing dinner plate behind them; the stand before the window with its pots of heliotrope and rose geraniums, and the red and gold lacquered box that held Laura Morrill's sewing; the conch shell for a doorstop; the ship model on the shelf; the black screen with the strange gold birds that stood before the couch. These were things she *knew* as you could only know the things you had dusted and handled; she would never forget them because the feel of them would always linger in her hands.

When Mrs. Morrill came back, she put into Greta's hands a little gray Persian kitten. "Princess would like you to have one of her kittens to take home," she said.

The tiny soft thing snuggled sleepily into Greta's arms. It was as gray and as gentle as a breath of fog, but it brought only dismay to Greta. She remembered the piece of strawberry pie that Mrs. Morrill had given her on the day of her very first visit. What would happen?

"Must I—must I take it?" she asked. There were tears in her eyes and it was hard to keep her voice steady.

"You'll always be glad you did, Greta, and you'll love her. Now, my dear—" She opened the door. Greta forgot she was twelve and almost grown up. She threw herself, kitten and all, into Mrs. Morrill's arms and clung to her like a much smaller girl than she was. Then she stumbled out into the fog.

"Safe passage," Mrs. Morrill said quietly, "safe passage for all the years ahead!" She gave Greta a last smile and sent her, comforted and confident, on her way. Greta stopped only long enough to pick up her sweater and wrap it around the kitten. She turned up the Old Road toward home without once looking back.

Beyond Old Man Himion's, Walter Addington stood waiting. Greta held up the kitten for him to see. "Can I keep it? I—I mean, *will* it keep?" She almost whispered the words.

Father reached into his pocket and when he pulled out his hand he kept it closed for a minute. The kitten reached out an impudent little paw and slapped at his closed fist. Father looked at the kitten and laughed. "All right," he said and opened his hand wide. On his palm lay an odd little knife. The kitten reached for it, but Father drew his hand back. "I suppose you think you've a right to it," he said, "but you're wrong. I've had that knife since my twelfth birthday and I aim to keep it as long as I live. No wisp of a kitten is going to bat it down a crack in the rocks and lose it for me."

Greta caught her breath. "Did you get it at Blue Cove, Father?" she asked.

Her father nodded. "On my twelfth birthday."

Greta thought he wasn't going to say anything more but after a while he began again.

"I think you'll keep your kitten," he said at last very slowly. "On your twelfth birthday, Greta, you grow up, and you put away childish things. Sometimes you'll wish you hadn't because you put behind you so many things—happy and unhappy. But the next twelve years can be happier still, my girl, and the twelve after that. And try to remember this—none of the things you think you've lost on the way are *really lost*. Every one of them is folded around you—close."

"Then tomorrow there'll *only* be cellar holes—and always, from now on?" she asked slowly. Her father seemed to understand.

"Cellar holes, yes. But cellar holes and spruce thickets, and rocks piled high. Old Fundy beating on the shore, clouds blowing overhead, and the gulls mewing. The grandest spot of land on the continent—and your homeland. And back here on this side of the mountain there'll be a gray wisp of fur waiting to purr for you. This kitten should bring you a line of kittens that'll last as long as my knife," he ended.

Whether the magic lay in Father's words or in his understanding Greta did not know. But she felt her heart grow light. "I'll call her Wisp," she said happily, "because she's like the tiny wisps of fog that are left behind in shaded corners of the rocks, sometimes, when the sun burns off the rest. And, Father, your knife and my kitten—it's fun, isn't it, to have them and to *know?*"

"To know?" her father smiled. "Yes, it's fun, Greta, and all that lies ahead can be fun, too—the growing and the living."

"I'm glad I'm twelve and growing up," Greta thought, "no matter *what* I have to give up. But I'm going back over the mountain. All my life I'm going back to Blue Cove. I'll take Wisp and *her* kittens, and *their* kittens forever and forever. And I'll let them play in the cellar holes and nap on the stone doorsteps of Blue Cove."

She slipped her arm through her father's. With the kitten held close, they walked down the Old Road through the fog toward the lights of Little Valley and the years ahead.